PRAISE FOR *MIRIAM'S SECRET*

"In this heart-warm... ...
ship, Debby Waldm...
America's history of ... ...a nobos. As
Miriam grapples with keeping her friend's secret
or doing the right thing, Waldman adeptly brings
history alive, painting an engaging portrait of minor-
ities in a small town and showing that cultural
differences can bring people together."

—**Leanne Lieberman**,
author of *The Most Dangerous Thing*

"A wonderful, tantalizing and tender tale about
how, despite our differences, we all long for the same
things: friendship, connection and a sense
of purpose."

—**Monique Polak**,
award-winning author of *What World Is Left*

"An endearing story about the power of acceptance."

—**Marsha Forchuk Skrypuch**,
award-winning author of *Making Bombs for Hitler*

Debby Waldman

MIRIAM'S SECRET

ORCA BOOK PUBLISHERS

Library and Archives Canada Cataloguing in Publication

Waldman, Debby, author
Miriam's secret / Debby Waldman.

Issued also in print and electronic formats.
ISBN 978-1-4598-1425-7 (softcover).—ISBN 978-1-4598-1426-4 (PDF).—
ISBN 978-1-4598-1427-1 (epub)

I. Title.
PS8645.A457M57 2017   jc813'.6   C2017-900846-3
C2017-900847-1

First published in the United States, 2017
Library of Congress Control Number: 2017933017

Summary: In this middle-grade novel, Miriam discovers a young girl hiding in the barn while she's spending Passover at her grandparents' farm.

Orca Book Publishers is dedicated to preserving the environment and has printed this book on Forest Stewardship Council® certified paper.

Orca Book Publishers gratefully acknowledges the support for its publishing programs provided by the following agencies: the Government of Canada through the Canada Book Fund and the Canada Council for the Arts, and the Province of British Columbia through the BC Arts Council and the Book Publishing Tax Credit.

Edited by Tanya Trafford
Cover artwork by Scott Plumbe
Author photo by Curtis Trent

ORCA BOOK PUBLISHERS
www.orcabook.com

Printed and bound in Canada.

20 19 18 17 • 4 3 2 1

*To my grandparents, Velvel (William) Chernoff
and Dora (Eva) Rollband Chernoff, and
Harris Zvi Waldman and Sarah Papkin Waldman—
may their memories be for a blessing.*

ONE

Miriam was startled awake. Her room was shaking, the window next to her bed rattling like chattering teeth. A long, eerie whistle reminded her that she wasn't in Brooklyn anymore.

Sitting up, she pushed the curtains apart, expecting to see a giant lifting her grandparents' farmhouse off the ground. But the moonlight revealed only the lights of a caboose. She watched it disappear down the snow-covered train tracks. The night fell still and silent once again.

The next time Miriam opened her eyes, sunlight was leaking through the curtains. Her grandmother was standing by the bed, smiling down at her.

Bubby had a smudge of flour on her cheek, and her soft gray hair was coming loose from her bun.

"Rise and shine, Miri," she said cheerfully. "I've got your breakfast all ready."

When Bubby went back down the stairs, Miriam knelt on the bed and pushed the curtains apart again. The train tracks cut a path through the snow, stretching from the bridge over the road at one end of the yard all the way to the woods at the other. Letting the curtains fall back together, she turned to the closet where Bubby had stored her clothes. As she pulled on her dress and wool stockings, she kept an eye on the window, wondering when the next train would come.

Bubby had set a bowl of oatmeal at the kitchen table. Miriam looked around the room. She had never seen such a big kitchen—it was almost as big as her entire apartment back home. She wondered if Bubby and Zayde were lonely eating at that big table every day, all by themselves, surrounded by empty chairs.

She thought back to her breakfast the day before with Mama, Papa and Bubby at the cozy table in their apartment in New York. Mama had served her favorites—warm, chewy *bialys*, soft cheese and smoked whitefish.

"What do you think Mama and Papa are doing right this minute?" Miriam asked her grandmother as she stirred a spoonful of molasses into her oatmeal.

Bubby looked at the clock over the sink. It was almost eight. "I imagine they're getting ready to board the ship. They're setting sail today."

"I wish I could go with them," Miriam said wistfully. She wiped her nose with the back of her hand.

Bubby pulled a handkerchief from her apron pocket and passed it to Miriam. "It's not a journey for a young girl," she said.

"Gabriel and Rafael are *babies*," Miriam said. "Why do they get to make the journey?"

"They have to," Bubby reminded her. "It's the only way for them to get to America."

"Uncle Avram can bring them," Miriam insisted. "He's coming to America too. So why do Mama and Papa have to go?"

She knew why. Mama had told her so many times, she couldn't count. Bubby gave the same answer. "Your uncle Avram can't take care of two babies himself. He needs your mama to help him, and she can't travel that far alone."

Miriam still didn't understand. It wasn't as if Mama would get lost. All she had to do was board a ship to Germany and from Germany travel by train to the Old Country. Uncle Avram would meet her at the station in Borisov, and together they would bring Gabriel and Rafael back to New York. Papa couldn't help with the babies, so why did he even need to go?

"Your mama has never been to Borisov, Miriam," Bubby reminded her. "She doesn't speak Russian."

Papa had lived in Borisov until he'd moved to New York fourteen years earlier. A cousin of a cousin of a cousin had found him a job operating a pushcart. Cousin Mendel also had a pushcart— he sold paper and pencils. Papa sold buttons and thread, which is how he had met Mama.

Your mama needed pewter buttons. Not silver. Not gold. Not tin. They had to be pewter, Papa told Miriam whenever she asked to hear the story, which was often. *What did I know from pewter?*

He knew from pewter, Mama would say, laughing. *He just pretended.*

Miriam liked the idea of Papa being so in love with Mama that he purposely did not try too hard to find the special buttons, to keep her coming back to the pushcart.

By the time I found those buttons, your mama was as in love with me as I was with her, Papa said proudly.

Now Papa and Mendel ran a dry-goods store together. Mendel had brought the rest of his family to America. Papa wanted to do the same, but his parents—Miriam's other grandparents—had died soon after he left Borisov, within a few months of each other. His brother Avram had never really wanted to leave the Old Country. Uncle Avram only changed his mind when his wife, Tante Chaya, died of a fever two months after the babies were born. Miriam said a silent prayer to keep Papa and Mama and Uncle Avram and the twins safe and get them back to America as soon as possible. It was her fifth such prayer of the morning.

"If only Lindbergh's flying machine was big enough for an entire family," Miriam said with a sigh.

Bubby reached across the table and patted Miriam's hand. "A ship is much safer than a flying machine, Miri," she said.

"But a ship is so much slower," Miriam said. She remembered when Papa had shown her the newspaper story about Charles Lindbergh flying across the ocean from Long Island to Paris in only thirty-three hours. It was her eighth birthday, and Papa had brought home the newspaper as a keepsake. She still had that newspaper, in a trunk at the foot of her bed with her other treasures.

"I thought you were excited about coming to stay with us on the farm," Bubby said. "You can have all kinds of adventures here."

Mama had whispered almost the same thing into Miriam's ear the previous day. *The farm is full of surprises. You'll be so busy, the time will fly. Papa and I will be home with Uncle Avram and your cousins before you know it.*

Bubby was still talking. "…so much you can do here that you can't in a city full of cars and sidewalks and buildings and noise. How can you sleep with such noise? Here, it's so peaceful and quiet."

Miriam shook her head. "No it's not," she said. "I heard a train last night."

"Ach, the train," Bubby said, leaning back in her chair. "You'll get used to it. By next week you'll sleep right through it."

"Does it come every night?" Miriam asked.

"Trains go up and down that track every night and every day," Bubby replied. "They travel from Canada to Florida and everywhere in between."

"Like Utica? And New York City?" Miriam asked.

Bubby nodded.

Miriam was confused. After breakfast the day before, she and Bubby had climbed aboard a train at Grand Central Station in Manhattan. When they stepped off, in Utica, it was time for dinner.

Zayde had met them at the station. Then he'd driven them to the farm in his pickup truck. The ride was so long that Miriam had been fast asleep when they arrived.

"Why didn't we take that train yesterday?" Miriam asked. "Why did we have to get off in Utica?"

"Only freight trains travel on that track," Bubby said with a smile. "Freight trains carry things, not people."

"What kinds of things?" Miriam asked.

"All kinds of things—clothes, food, pots and pans, even stoves and iceboxes."

"Why not people?" Miriam asked.

"The cars don't have seats," Bubby said. "Just big empty spaces to hold the freight. Imagine sitting on a hard floor all the way from New York."

"I don't think I would like that," Miriam said.

Bubby nodded. "I don't think so either."

TWO

"Come along," Bubby said after Miriam finished her breakfast. "You and I have a job to do."

Miriam hoped it was something you could do inside, like making a cake. But Mama had warned her that most of the work at the farm was outside—picking vegetables, pulling weeds, letting cows in and out of the barn.

It was so cold right now that Miriam couldn't imagine a vegetable growing, or even a weed. And she hadn't seen any cows. She could barely see beyond the snow outside the windows.

Until the day before, Miriam hadn't been to the farm since she was a baby. She'd lived all eleven years of her life in Brooklyn. When Mama wanted vegetables, she and Miriam walked to the greengrocer, next to the bakery at the end of the block. For eggs they went to the market across the street. They didn't have to go to a store for milk—a milkman delivered it in glass bottles, right to their building.

Earlier that morning Zayde had come back from the barn with a dented metal pail full of milk, *fresh from the cow*, he said. It was warm and creamy, topped with a layer of froth.

When Bubby wanted eggs, she walked to the chicken coop. "Put on your coat and boots," she said to Miriam. "It's not far, but we don't want your feet getting wet."

The chicken coop was across the yard, at the edge of the woods that bordered the farm. As Miriam and her grandmother crunched along a well-worn path in the snow, Miriam counted the buildings. Just off to the side of the house was the outhouse, which Miriam had visited before breakfast and vowed not to use again until the weather warmed up. There was a chamber pot in her room.

She hadn't wanted to use it, for fear she might spill the contents on the way downstairs to empty it. But she was now willing to take the risk. Anything would be better than sitting bare-bottomed in a wooden shed when the wind was howling outside.

Not far from the outhouse were the icehouse and the woodshed. Beyond the chicken coop stood a big red barn, a smaller red barn, a one-story building and a round white tube nearly as tall as the New York skyscrapers Miriam could see from her bedroom window back home. Off in the distance was a large, partly built wooden frame.

"That's the new barn," said Bubby when she noticed Miriam staring. "The hired men will finish it before spring."

Miriam wondered why the farm needed a new barn, but she didn't have time to ask. They had reached the coop. The door wasn't much taller than she was. To fit through, Bubby had to stoop. Her chin almost bumped her knees.

It was dark in there. And the stink was worse than anything Miriam had smelled, even on garbage day. She pinched her nose.

"You'll need both your hands to gather the eggs," Bubby said. "Breathe through your mouth. It won't smell so bad."

Miriam tried to focus in the dim light. She could see shelves lined with shallow wooden boxes filled with straw. On top of each box sat a chicken. All of them stared at Miriam but never moved a feather.

"What eggs?" Miriam asked. "I don't see any eggs."

"They're under the chickens," Bubby explained.

"So how do we get them?"

"Like this." Bubby nudged the chicken in front of her. Quickly, and ever so gently, she pushed against its fat, feathered side. The chicken tipped slightly to the left. Bubby reached under.

Her hand emerged cradling an egg. Or, at least, Miriam thought it was an egg. Its brown shell was speckled with dirt and straw. It looked nothing like a clean, smooth Brooklyn egg.

Bubby seemed to know exactly what Miriam was thinking. "After we wash it, it will look just like the eggs your mama buys," she promised. "And it will taste even better!"

Squatting in front of the lower shelf, she nudged the chicken nearest her. "It's your turn," she said.

Miriam dropped to her knees.

"That's your egg," Bubby said, pointing with her free hand. "Grab it."

Miriam reached. The chicken turned its head. Miriam snatched her hand back. "It's going to bite me!"

"It's not," Bubby assured her.

"How do you know?"

"Chickens don't have teeth," she said.

"Then how do they eat?" Miriam asked.

"Oh, they eat," Bubby replied. "Don't you worry about the chickens."

Miriam tried again. This time when her grandmother nudged the hen, Miriam was able to scoop up the egg. Then she tried doing it without Bubby's help. Soon the basket was full. As they walked back to the house, Miriam counted. Fourteen eggs!

"Why do we need so many?" she asked.

"We have many mouths to feed," Bubby said. "Sometimes I don't even know how many."

That explained all the chairs around the table in the kitchen. "But I thought it was just you and me and Zayde."

"No, we have—" A train thundering down the tracks blew away the rest of Bubby's words. She continued toward the house, but Miriam stayed, staring.

Three big black barrels rolled out of one of the cars and landed on the snow. And then, even more amazing, the barrels uncoiled themselves. Then Miriam could see that they weren't barrels at all. They were men wearing long dark coats and felt hats.

Miriam ran as fast as she could into the house. "You said the trains carried things, not people!" she said to her grandmother. "But people got off the train! Come and see!"

She pulled Bubby to the front window. Zayde was out there now, and his dog, Mazel, was standing next to him, his long silky tail wagging in excitement, stirring up the snow.

Zayde and the men were nodding and talking like old friends. Miriam could tell they were all talking at the same time—their breath floated in front of their faces before it dissolved into the cold morning air.

"Who are they?" Miriam asked.

"They're hobos," Bubby explained. "Men who travel from place to place looking for work. Sometimes they don't have money to buy a train ticket. So they hide in empty freight cars and jump off where they think they can find work. And your zayde always hires them. Even if there isn't any work. He's got a soft heart."

"And you feed them?" Miriam asked. "That's why we need the eggs?"

"That's right," Bubby said. "I used my last eggs this morning, making breakfast for four hired men and Zayde before you even woke up. That's why you had oatmeal."

"Do the men eat here all the time? With us?"

Bubby nodded.

"Do they sleep in the house too?" She wondered where—the house didn't look that big.

"They sleep in the bunkhouse." Bubby pointed to the little building that Miriam had noticed on the way to collect the eggs. "They eat with us because they don't have time to cook."

"I help Mama cook dinner every night," Miriam said. "But there are only three of us, so we don't have to make very much. Do you have to make lots of food for the hired men?"

Bubby nodded solemnly. "They work hard— and they eat a lot."

"I think it would be fun to cook for lots of people," Miriam said. "I can help you! Can I help you?"

"That would be lovely," said Bubby. She reached down and hugged Miriam. "If you're as good at cooking as you are at gathering eggs, those hired men will be in for a real treat."

THREE

At lunchtime seven men followed Zayde into the house. They hung their coats in the front hall and left their boots on the rug under the coat hooks. Bubby had made the rug out of old rags.

The men were all dressed like Zayde, in denim pants with suspenders over faded plaid shirts. Miriam couldn't tell which ones had jumped off the train that morning. They were all younger than Zayde, with full heads of hair—blond, brown, black, even gray. When Zayde took off his cap, you could see he had only a few silver wires sticking straight up from his otherwise shiny head.

Some of the men had funny names like Stretch and Banjo. Some of them were black. They were all tall and broad-shouldered and looked as if they could easily pick up her much smaller grandfather and swing him around the kitchen the way Papa used to swing her.

Most of them were probably about as old as Papa, or older. Only the smallest and clearly the youngest of the men, Joe, didn't have deep lines etched into his face. His skin was dark and as smooth as a polished stone.

Joe reminded Miriam of the porter she'd met on the train the day before, but that man had been older than Joe, and louder. He had joked with Miriam as he helped her off the train, calling her "little lady" and warning her that Utica was "a speck of a town compared to New York City."

I'm going to Sangerfield, Miriam had explained, and the porter had thrown back his head and let out such a howl that for a moment Miriam had been frightened. Then she realized he was laughing, though she couldn't for the life of her figure out why. When he finally caught his breath, he'd said, *Sangerfield is too small to even count as a speck!* Bubby seemed to find that amusing, but it had made Miriam even more anxious.

When Joe caught Miriam looking at him, he quickly turned his attention back to his plate. Miriam wondered if he thought she was staring at the amount of food he was eating. His plate was swimming with stew, and he had helped himself to so many of Bubby's warm, fluffy rolls that some were falling into his lap.

She looked to see if Bubby had noticed, but Bubby was busy telling one of the men sitting near her that she had used water and yeast to make the rolls, not butter.

"That's a lot of fuss you go to," said the man— Miriam thought he might be Stretch. "My mama, she used to make buttermilk biscuits to sop up gravy. Flakiest biscuits you ever did taste, and she whipped them up in no time. Didn't have to knead them or nothing."

Was he saying that his mama's biscuits were nicer than Bubby's rolls?

"But yours are mighty fine too, ma'am," he said. As Bubby thanked him, he helped himself to the last one in the basket.

Miriam turned her attention back to Joe. He was the skinniest hired man at the table. That's probably why he ate so much. But if he ate that way all the time, Miriam thought to herself, he shouldn't be skinny. She wanted to smile at him. She wanted him to know that she would have taken even more rolls if she had to work all afternoon building a new barn, but Joe didn't meet her eyes for the rest of the meal.

"I got a little girl about your age," said Banjo, who was sitting on the other side of Miriam. He reached into his shirt pocket and pulled out a folded-up square of paper. He unfolded it to reveal a well-creased, faded photograph of a smiling girl. Her golden-blond hair hung in braids that nearly reached her waist. She was cradling a kitten.

"Her name's Meg," Banjo said. "That's her kitten, Jojo, though I expect Jojo's a full-grown cat by now."

"It's an awfully nice picture," Miriam said. Meg looked friendly. Miriam wondered if they could be friends. She'd never been friends with anyone who owned a kitten or even a cat. "Do they live nearby?"

Banjo shook his head. "Oh no, miss," he said. "Meg and her mama live in Kansas. That's days away on the train. I haven't seen them since last summer. I'm working for your grandpa to earn enough money so I can go back and be with them again."

"You've been here since last summer?" Miriam asked.

"Oh no. I just rolled off the train this morning," Banjo said. If Miriam hadn't seen it with her own eyes she would have thought "rolled off the train" was just an expression.

"But where were you before?" Miriam asked. "I mean, between summer and now?"

"Picked corn in Indiana, pecans in Georgia, baled hay in Pennsylvania. Played some music on street corners and made a few pennies that way. Done whatever I could to earn a buck to send back home."

"What kind of instrument do you play?" Miriam asked.

"See if you can guess," Banjo said. When he smiled, his eyes crinkled.

Miriam figured it out right away and felt foolish for asking such a silly question. But then she decided to play along. "The clarinet?" she said, trying not to laugh.

"Try again, miss," Banjo encouraged.

"The tuba?"

"Nope."

"The accordion?" Miriam's uncle Nathan, who lived in New York, played the accordion.

"Yessiree, you've got it!" Banjo said.

"I was joking!" Miriam said. "Why on earth are you called Banjo if you play the accordion?"

"I was joking too!" said Banjo, letting loose a belly laugh that caught the attention of everyone around the table. "I've been playing banjo since my hands was big enough to pluck the strings."

Miriam felt her face grow hot. She looked across the table. Even Joe was laughing. She took a deep breath and tried to join in. She still felt silly, but it was hard to resist that laughter for long.

Bubby served apple and blueberry pies for dessert, and once they'd had their fill, the men filed back out the door, thanking her for the meal. Zayde stayed behind. Miriam noticed him looking over at Bubby in a way that made her curious.

Zayde turned to Miriam, his dark eyes warm and inviting. "How would you like to come see the barn?" The way he said "vud" instead of "would" reminded Miriam of Papa. Zayde had lived in the Old Country until he was almost twenty years old, the same age Papa had been when he sailed to America. In the Old Country they spoke Yiddish at home and Russian in the marketplace. That's why they both talked funny. They learned to speak English when they were much older. Bubby had come to America when she was a baby. She sounded more like Mama, like Miriam.

Zayde winked at Bubby. Now Miriam was sure they had a secret. Maybe it was a surprise, like Mama had promised.

Miriam looked at her grandmother.

"Go ahead," Bubby said, smiling as she nodded toward the door. "Just stay out of trouble, the two of you."

FOUR

The barn was much bigger than the chicken coop—
nobody had to duck to get in the door. Zayde
stamped on the hard-packed dirt floor to get the
snow off his boots. Miriam stamped too. Mazel
shook his coat and wagged his tail.

Small, square windows high on the walls let in
enough light for Miriam to make out her grandfather and the dog. Beyond that were shadows,
silence and a smell that was hard to identify.
Miriam scrunched up her nose, trying to place
the odor, a mixture of sour milk and something
almost sweet.

Zayde pulled a string next to the door and the room brightened. Suspended by wires from low wooden beams were bare lightbulbs. Miriam could practically reach up and touch them. She wasn't sure what she had been expecting, but it wasn't this. The room seemed to stretch on forever. It was divided into thirds—a center aisle wide enough for a railway car, and two narrower sections on either side. The floor in the center aisle was made of wood. The aisles were strewn with dirty, matted straw.

"Where are the cows?" Miriam asked.

"They're out in the pasture," Zayde replied. "We'll go there another day. Or if you really want, you can come see them at milking time."

"Aren't they cold outside?" Miriam asked.

"They know how to stay warm," Zayde said. "They huddle together if they have to. But would you want to stay in here all day, not able to walk around or see the sunshine? At least outside they are free to move as they please."

He pointed to the long, narrow rows on either side of the center aisle. "When they're in here, they have to be lined up next to each other."

Wooden, fence-like structures ran the length of each row, but unlike regular fences, they had rails only on top. If they were fences, they didn't look as if they'd be useful. Anything smaller than a giraffe or an elephant could have escaped with ease.

Miriam pointed to them. "What are those?"

"Stanchions," her grandfather replied. "They help keep the cows in place at milking time."

"How many cows do you have?"

"Almost a hundred. And one bull."

"Why only one?" Miriam asked.

"You only need one bull," Zayde said.

"He must be lonely," Miriam said.

"He does just fine," Zayde said. "He's got all the cows to keep him company."

At the end of the rows was a series of doors. Most led to stalls, but the one that Zayde stopped in front of opened into a small room about the size of Miriam's bedroom in the farmhouse. Inside was a wood-burning stove and a box so big that Miriam wondered if something lived in it. Zayde lifted the cover and reached in. Miriam stood on her toes to peer inside. The box was full of fat brown seeds the size of rice.

"What's that?" she asked as Zayde dipped a pail into the box and came out with it filled nearly to overflowing.

"Oats." Zayde set the pail on the floor.

"This doesn't look like oatmeal," Miriam said, picking up a handful. It felt heavier than the rice Mama kept in a jar in the kitchen.

"These are whole oats," Zayde explained. "Oatmeal is made from what's inside."

"So we're going to make oatmeal?" Miriam asked.

Zayde laughed his merry laugh and shook his head. "These are for Betsy," he said.

"Who's Betsy?"

"Come along," Zayde said. "I'll introduce you."

He unlatched the door to the stall across the hall and held it open. Miriam kicked through the hay at the entrance and then stopped abruptly. In front of her stood a butterscotch-colored horse so tall that Miriam's head barely reached its shoulders. Its hooves were as wide as dinner plates.

"This is Betsy," Zayde said.

Betsy tossed her head up and down as if nodding a greeting, but it was soon apparent that she was more interested in the oats than in the visitors. Pulling back her lips, she moved her head toward the bucket in Zayde's hands. Her teeth made Miriam think of the rubber erasers she used back at PS 131, her school in New York. Unlike erasers, though, Betsy's teeth were enormous, and they looked hard, like something that could crush bones.

Miriam backed away.

"She won't hurt you," Zayde said gently. "She only wants her food."

He walked to the back of the stall and leaned over a wooden fence about a foot away from the wall. Then he turned the bucket upside down and emptied it. The sound the oats made when they landed reminded Miriam of the last time Mama had made popcorn, when she'd accidentally spilled the kernels on the kitchen floor. "Why are you throwing her food down there?" Miriam asked.

"It's a trough," Zayde said.

"What's a troff?"

Zayde boosted her up so she could hang over the rail and see what was on the other side. What she had thought was a fence was the front of a long, shallow wooden box. She reached into it and felt the oats that had settled at the bottom. The box was about as deep as her arm was long.

"It's Betsy's cupboard and table at the same time," Zayde explained. "It's where she gets her food when she can't go outside to eat grass."

He looked up at the ceiling and pointed. Above them was an opening slightly wider than the trough. "That's the hayloft," he said. "We can drop hay from there right down here."

Miriam looked up again, wondering if hay might fall right this minute. Two brown eyes stared down at her.

Before she could stop herself, she screamed. The noise startled Betsy, who whinnied loudly and stamped her massive hooves. Zayde picked up Miriam and hurried her out of the stall.

"*Oy vavoy!*" he said, setting her down on the floor. "What made you scream like that?"

"Someone was up there!" Miriam's voice was shaky.

"In the hayloft?"

Miriam nodded.

"The men are often up there," Zayde assured her. "They need to get the hay down for the cows."

"But the cows are out in the field," Miriam said. "Why would someone be getting them hay now?"

"To bring out to the field," Zayde said. "All that snow—they can't get at the grass, so we bring them hay. Whoever was up there must have heard our voices and got curious and looked down. You get curious, don't you?"

Miriam nodded. She didn't ask any more questions. Zayde was so certain that it was one of the men. She'd only seen them for a second, but it had been long enough to be certain that those eyes did not belong to one of the men. She wished she had looked longer instead of screaming. Next time, she promised herself, she would be brave. Next time she would stare right back.

FIVE

"There's something else I want to show you," Zayde said outside Betsy's stall.

Miriam was still thinking about what she had just seen. "How do you get into the hayloft?" she asked.

"There's a ladder up there." Zayde pointed to the middle of the barn. "And there's a staircase outside, around the side."

"Can I go up there?" Miriam asked.

"It's not for girls," Zayde said. "Come."

A pile of wooden crates was heaped by the back entrance. Zayde took one and carried it to the back of the stall across from Betsy's. Except for the hay all over the floor, the stall was empty. Miriam looked up at the ceiling. There was an opening, but no one looking down at her. Still, she couldn't shake the feeling that she was being watched. She looked at Zayde. He was smiling at her.

Slowly Miriam turned around, inspecting the entire stall. She spent an extra-long time scanning the narrow opening to the hayloft. "There's nobody—nothing in here," she said finally.

"Oh, but there is," Zayde said.

For just a minute she was frightened again, but when she saw the playful look on her grandfather's face she knew he wasn't talking about eyes in the hayloft. Putting a hand on her shoulder, he directed her toward the trough.

"Stand on that," he said, pointing to the crate he'd carried into the stall.

Miriam did as she was told. When she peered into the trough, she almost yelled again, this time because she was so excited.

Seven kittens clustered around a solemn-looking mother cat. The mother was the same color as the straw lining the trough. Three of the kittens looked like her, and four were almost all white except for some black around their paws and eyes. Some of them looked like bank robbers. Others looked as if they'd forgotten to put on all of their socks.

"They were born about a week ago," Zayde said. "Just in time for your visit."

None were much bigger than Miriam's hands. Their eyes were barely open. They were falling over each other trying to get to their mother, who rested, as still as a stuffed animal, on her straw bed.

Miriam turned to her grandfather. "Can I play with them?"

"Soon," Zayde said. "They should be big enough by next week."

The next question escaped Miriam's mouth before she'd had a chance to even think what she was asking. "Can I have one?" As soon as she had spoken, she scolded herself. How greedy she sounded! "I didn't mean to be impertinent," she added.

"You weren't," Zayde said. "Your grandmother and I thought you might like one for yourself, at least while you are here. When they're old enough to leave their mother, you can pick whichever one you want and bring it into the house to live with you."

Miriam thought of Jojo, the kitten in the picture that Banjo had showed her at lunch. Banjo had been gone for six months before Meg's kitten had turned into a cat. Miriam didn't have that much time. "Next week?" she asked.

"Oh no," Zayde said. "They'll be big enough to play with next week, but they won't be ready to leave their mama that soon. Around Passover, I would think."

"But won't I be back home by then?" Miriam asked.

Zayde shook his head. "That's only six weeks from now. Your mama and papa won't be back that soon. You'll spend Passover here with us."

Passover was Miriam's favorite holiday. The weeklong festival started with a *seder*. Miriam and Mama and Papa celebrated with Mendel, Papa's business partner. Mendel's mother, Tante Malka, had an apartment big enough to fit all of Mendel's brothers and sisters and their families. Everyone gathered around the dinner table to hear the story of how the Israelites escaped from slavery in Egypt. It took hours to tell. Usually Miriam and the other children were asleep by the time the special meal and story ended.

She didn't remember Mama telling her she would have to spend Passover on the farm.

"Don't look so sad, Miri," Zayde said. "The seder will be extra special because you'll be here."

Miriam couldn't imagine a seder on the farm, with only Bubby and Zayde and Mazel and a kitten.

"Can I name one of the kittens Moses?" she asked. "He was the hero of the Passover story because he led the Israelites across the Red Sea, to freedom in the Promised Land."

"Yes, Miri, I know," Zayde said, chuckling. "You can name the kittens whatever you'd like."

"What's the mama cat's name?"

"MC, short for Mouse Catcher."

Miriam studied the wiggly kittens. "That's Moses," she said, pointing to an orange kitten with a striped tail. He was off to the side, watching the others crowding each other to get close to their mother.

There wasn't enough space around MC for all her kittens. Two huddled together, patiently waiting their turn. Watching them made Miriam think of Anna and Ida, Mendel's daughters. They were sisters, but they almost never fought. They were more like friends, and they were Miriam's best friends. Even though she had said goodbye to them only two days ago, she already missed them dearly.

Anna had light hair, and Ida's was dark like Miriam's, but even more curly. "I'm going to name that one Anna," Miriam said, pointing to the straw-colored kitten. Pointing to the one with two black paws, she said, "That one's Ida."

If she couldn't have her human friends on the farm, kittens would have to do.

SIX

At PS 131, Miriam was in sixth grade. At the farm, she had school in the kitchen. Bubby used books that Mama had sent so Miriam could practice mathematics, spelling, penmanship and recitation. For reading, Bubby gave her a well-worn book, *The Railway Children*.

"Your mama used to like this one," her grandmother said. "It's about two sisters and their brother who move from London to the country with their mother after their father goes away. I thought you might like it."

Miriam flipped through the pages. "Why does the father go away?" she asked.

"If I tell you it will spoil the story," Bubby said. "You'll have to read it yourself to find out."

"Now?" Miriam said.

"If you like."

Miriam carried the book into the front room and sank down into the sofa next to the window. Roberta, or "Bobbie," Peter and Phyllis certainly had a nice life—a big house, lots of toys, good food, parents who played with them, and a nanny, a cook and a housekeeper who did all the housework. They didn't have to do anything all day except play with each other.

"How are you liking the book so far?" Bubby asked when Miriam went back into the kitchen after a while.

"It made me homesick," Miriam admitted.

"Homesick? It takes place in England. How can you be homesick for a place you've never visited?"

"I miss Anna and Ida," she explained. "Phil and Peter and Bobbie have each other to play with, so they don't get lonely."

"Oh, I see," said Bubby. "Well, how about writing a letter to your cousins? That's a good way to practice your penmanship."

March 4, 1930

Dear Anna and Ida,

It is my second full day at Bubby and Zayde's. We got here so late on Sunday night that I was already asleep. Zayde had to carry me upstairs to my bedroom, and I slept the whole time! My window overlooks the train tracks, but the closest train station is almost twenty miles away, so we had a long trip from the station to the farm. Zayde owns a pickup truck. The ride was very bumpy, but not as loud as the subway.

You would not believe how much empty space there is on the farm. There are no tall buildings, so you can see forever. The tallest building isn't even really a building. It's called a silo. That's where Zayde keeps the grain for the cows and the horse. The horse's name is Betsy.

There is also a cat in the barn. Her name is MC for Mouse Catcher, and she has seven kittens! Zayde is letting me name them. So far I have named one Moses, because he is the leader. And... I named one Anna and one Ida! Because I miss you. And there is nobody to play with at Bubby and

Zayde's except for the kittens. But they don't talk. They just meow and purr.

Have you been to the cinema? There is no cinema here. Write and tell me what films you have seen. I have to go now because Zayde is going to take me into town to mail this. It will be my first trip to town. Very exciting!

Your cousin,
Miriam

Sangerfield wasn't really a town. As the porter had said, it was more of a speck. The closest town was Waterville, and it wasn't much more than a speck. Sangerfield only had one main street and one stoplight. None of the buildings was more than three stories tall.

The people didn't rush past each other the way they did back home. They walked slowly. Some just hung out in front of Bert's Café and the Dew Drop Inn to chat.

Some greeted Zayde with "Morning, Bill" and a tip of their hat. Some said something that sounded like, "It's Billy that's you."

"Why do they say that?" Miriam asked, scattering snow on the sidewalk with her bright red boots.

"Don't people say good morning in Brooklyn?" Zayde sounded surprised.

"Of course!" Miriam said. "But those people said, *It's Billy that's you*. That seems strange."

"They said what?" Zayde asked.

"*It's Billy that's you*. Don't they *know* it's you?"

Zayde started laughing so hard he had to stop walking. When he finally found his voice again, he said, "Oh, Miri! They didn't say, *It's Billy that's you*. They said, *It's Billy the Jew*."

Miriam frowned. "Why don't they just say hello?"

"That's how some people do say hello," Zayde explained.

He took Miriam's hand, and they walked on. "Mr. Zadowa owns the dry-goods store," he said, pointing as they passed a window filled with everything from shovels to fabric. "When they see him, they say, *It's Jerry the Pole*, because he comes from Poland. And Mr. Wegmann, from the butcher shop? They say to him, *It's Gunter the German*, because—"

"He comes from Germany?"

"No, his father came from Germany. But you get the idea."

"Why does it matter?" Miriam asked.

"Why does what matter?" Zayde said.

"Where someone comes from?" In Brooklyn, nobody cared where you were from. If they knew you, they said hello. If they didn't, they didn't say anything.

"That is a good question, Miri," Zayde said. He paused. "I suppose it's because this is a very small town, much smaller than Brooklyn. When someone new appears, everyone notices."

"But you *do* live here," Miriam pointed out. "You've lived here since Mama was a girl. They should know who you are."

"To them, I'm still a greenhorn from the Old Country," Zayde said. "Most people here—their grandparents and great-grandparents and great-great-grandparents also lived here. They've been here almost as long as that tree."

He pointed across the street to a huge bare tree in the churchyard. Miriam could see that it was old—it was taller than the farmhouse. With its branches spreading over the street, it was wider too. But still she didn't understand.

"They feel as if they own the place, and it's their job to keep track of everybody," Zayde explained.

"If you had stayed in the Old Country, would you feel as if you owned your town?" Miriam asked.

Zayde laughed again, but it wasn't his usual merry laugh. "Things were very different there," he said, his voice turning serious. "That's why I came here."

SEVEN

The days settled into a routine. After breakfast Zayde and the men headed off to work, and Miriam and Bubby cleared the table and washed and dried the dishes. When the kitchen was clean, Miriam began her lessons. Sometimes Bubby sat with her, to give her a spelling test or listen as she recited "Paul Revere's Ride," which she wanted to memorize for her school's year-end assembly in June.

While Miriam practiced her penmanship or worked on arithmetic or went into the front room to catch up on the latest adventures of the Railway Children, Bubby peeled potatoes and carrots and chopped onions for lunch, usually a stew or soup, or sliced apples for a cake or pie. There was always something to do—cooking, dusting, sweeping, laundry.

At eleven forty-five, no matter what Miriam was doing, lessons ended. She set the table while Bubby finished preparing the noon meal. When the men returned to the house, everyone ate together. Then they trooped back outside, no matter the weather, and Miriam and Bubby cleaned up. Depending on what Bubby had planned, sometimes the preparation for dinner began as soon as lunch was over. But Bubby made time to accompany Miriam to visit the kittens nearly every day. Even then, though, she brought something with her to do, mending or knitting.

Zayde had told Bubby about the eyes in the hayloft. He'd turned it into a funny story, making it seem as if Miriam hadn't been scared, just startled. So good was he at storytelling that the first time Miriam returned to the barn with Bubby, she was nearly convinced that there was nothing to be scared about. Cradling Anna and Ida against her coat, she stared into the opening above the trough, daring the eyes to appear, determined not to scream if (or when) they did.

But the only eyes looking down were Bart's, and she knew right away that it was him. He called out, "Hello," then threw down some hay bales so that Miriam and Bubby did not have to sit on the floor. Then he threw down a few more for Miriam to play with.

"I have a little boy back home," Bart said. "He loves to build forts. See if you can make something dandy with these."

One day Miriam built a room for the kittens. The next day she made a maze. Moses was the first to discover that he could jump out of the maze instead of wandering through it.

The others were either too timid or more interested in playing with Bubby's yarn. When Miriam dangled a long strand in front of them, they danced on their hind legs, waving their front paws like stubby, furry hands as they fought to grab at the wool.

Back in the house, Miriam got into the habit of writing letters twice a week. On Tuesdays she wrote to Anna and Ida, and on Thursdays she wrote to Mama and Papa.

March 11, 1930

Dear Anna and Ida,

I wish I could go see the new Marx Brothers movie with you. Tell me all about it! Maybe we can act it out when I come home.

The kittens are getting bigger. Last week I got to play with them for the first time. I tried to put Anna and Ida into the pocket of my dress, but they were not pleased with their new quarters. I guess I would not like to be in someone's pocket either.

There are actually quite a few people on the farm—it's not just me and Bubby and Zayde and kittens and cows and a horse. That's because the farm is growing. When Mama was my age, the farm was smaller, and Zayde didn't need so much help.

The men he hires to work for him are hobos. They ride trains, looking for work. They say that they "ride the rails." They always come to this farm because they know Zayde will give them jobs.

They live in a bunkhouse, but they eat breakfast, lunch and dinner in the kitchen with us.

One of the hired men, Bart, carved me a checkerboard and checkers. On the other side of the board is another game called backgammon. Bart taught me how to play. I am getting very good at it. I beat him two times last night after dinner.

I cannot believe that Purim is almost here. Remember last year, when we all dressed up as Queen Esther? I won't be dressing up this year. The closest synagogue is miles away in Utica, and we never go there because it takes so long and there is too much to do here on the farm. But today Bubby and I are going to make her famous hamantaschen. (She says they are famous. I am not sure where or why they are famous, but yum anyway!)

Write soon and tell me if you have learned any new games.

Love,

Miriam

While Miriam was writing her letter, Bubby prepared the ingredients for the *hamantaschen*.

After lunch she and Miriam tied on matching aprons and began to assemble the pastries.

"Did you teach Mama how to make *mohn?*" Miriam asked, helping herself to a spoonful of the filling.

"Of course I did," Bubby said. "Doesn't this mohn taste the same as hers?"

Miriam reached her spoon into the bowl for a second taste. Bubby stopped her and handed her a clean spoon. "Use this," she said.

Miriam licked the spoon, savoring the sweet, grainy texture. "It's just as good," she said.

"No more tastes," said Bubby, laughing. "If we run out, we won't have enough to fill the hamantaschen."

"Can't we use jam?" Miriam asked. "Sometimes when we run out of mohn, that's what we do."

Bubby smiled and began rolling out the dough. "We won't run out if you stop eating it now."

Just as she did back home, Miriam used a drinking glass to cut circles in the dough. Into each circle she carefully spooned a generous dot of the filling.

"Perfect," Bubby said. "Do you remember how to close them up?"

"I think so," Miriam said. She folded part of the circle toward the middle and pinched the edges into corners, forming a triangle with the filling peeking through. "Like this?"

"Very good," Bubby said.

After dinner on Erev Purim, after the men had sampled the hamantaschen and returned to their bunkhouse, Zayde read the story of Esther to Miriam and Bubby. This year it seemed different, and not only because Miriam wasn't hearing it in a synagogue surrounded by friends and neighbors. Tonight she snuggled up on a sofa in a farmhouse, her head resting on her grandmother's shoulder.

For the first time, she could imagine what it must have been like to be Esther, alone in a new place with only a close relative for company. She knew it was just a story, and that sometimes in stories people seemed more heroic than they were in real life. But still, it impressed her that Esther never seemed scared. She was an orphan married to a king, and she couldn't even see him unless he sent her an invitation. But she was willing to take a chance, to just appear in his room to tell him that his chief aide was a villain. Miriam wondered whether she would have the courage, if she were in the same position, to go against the rules to do the right thing. She hoped so.

EIGHT

About a week after Purim, Bubby stood on her stepstool, pulling an enormous pot down from a shelf in the storage room. "I'm afraid I can't visit the kittens today, Miri," she said. "I have too many chores."

"Do you want me to stay and help?" Miriam asked. She knew she was supposed to help—that's what Mama had said. But she also wanted to see the kittens.

"Not today," Bubby said. "You go to the barn and play."

"By myself?" Miriam hadn't been to the barn alone. She had never been anywhere alone, unless you counted her bedroom at night, but even then a grown-up was close by.

"You won't be alone," Bubby reminded her. "You'll have seven kittens and a cat to keep you company. And Zayde might stop by to say hello. If you get lonely, you can come back here."

They were in the front hall now. Miriam had pulled on one boot when she stopped and looked up at her grandmother again. "I can stay and help you," she said. "I don't have to see the kittens today." She bent over to pull off the boot, but Bubby put her hand on Miriam's, stopping her.

"There's nothing to be afraid of," she reassured Miriam. "If I thought there was, I wouldn't let you go."

～

Miriam pushed open the heavy barn door and squinted. It was so bright outside that the barn seemed unusually dark. "Hello!" she called out, but no one responded.

Some afternoons when she and Bubby played with the kittens, the men were in the loft, working.

She would hear them, their heavy footsteps beating a rhythm overhead, and never give it a second thought. Today, even the faintest noise made her want to run back to the farmhouse.

She had never realized how many sounds there were in the barn. When she visited with Bubby, either she or Bubby was always talking. Their voices drowned out everything else. Now, alone in the entryway, she heard faint rustling, swishing, scratching—a symphony of sounds. It was not clear what they were or where they were coming from. And suddenly, instead of feeling cold from the air seeping in through the cracks in the door behind her, Miriam felt a wave of heat from her forehead to her toes.

Don't be scared, she told herself as she reached for the string by the door and turned on the lights. She hurried down the center aisle, kicking at loose pieces of hay. When she neared the stall next to the one with the kittens, she skidded to a stop. Something was rustling in the hay on the other side of the door. This stall was supposed to be empty. She inched closer to the door. Whatever was inside let out a low, whiny moan. It didn't sound human, but it definitely wasn't a kitten.

Stop being such a scaredy-cat, she thought.

She pushed the stall doors open so hard they banged against the walls and bounced closed and then open again, like enormous wooden hands clapping in slow motion. Taking a deep breath, she caught the doors on the backswing and held them open. Then she walked into the stall.

There, standing in the center, was a mother cow nursing a newborn. Miriam was so surprised she started to laugh. She had been afraid of a cow. What a funny story that would make for Bubby and Zayde! The cow's name was Corky—she remembered now that Zayde had spoken about the calf the previous night at dinner. He had named it Pickle.

Pickle was a noisy eater, slurping and swishing. Miriam, who loved baby animals, was tempted to pat her, but she didn't want to upset Corky, who was eyeing her in a way that made Miriam feel uncomfortable. As she left the stall, she got the same feeling she'd had that first day in the barn with Zayde, that something—or someone—was watching her.

She turned toward the stall with the kittens. Bandit and Pirate, whom Miriam had named for the black markings on their faces, were batting at each other. Moses had climbed on top of a pile of bales that Miriam had made into a tower. He was cleaning himself. First he licked one paw, then the other. The largest white kitten, the one with black markings on three of his paws, was stalking the smallest, straw-colored kitten.

"You're such a bully, Socks," Miriam said, bending over to poke the kitten with a piece of straw. "Leave Star alone!"

Sinking to her knees, she scooped up Anna and Ida, who squirmed frantically until she loosened her grip and they escaped to the floor.

"Some friends you are," she said, watching them disappear under the trough.

She flattened herself on the floor to watch them. "Where's your mother?" Right on cue, MC appeared from the corner near Corky and Pickle's stall. She slunk under the trough to join the two kittens.

Miriam rolled onto her back and looked at the opening to the hayloft. Remembering the fright she'd had on her first day in the barn, she balled her hands into fists, trying to keep calm. But the opening was as dark and quiet as ever.

Standing up, she brushed off her coat, turned to the tower of hay bales and studied the kittens. She still wasn't sure which one to keep, but she doubted it would be Anna or Ida. How could she choose one over the other? She considered changing their names—it would be easier to separate them if they weren't named after her friends. Then again, the way they kept running away from her together, they didn't seem to like her all that much. Bandit was probably a better choice. Or Pirate.

"Or you," she said, reaching for Star. Star used to be the shyest kitten, skittering away whenever Miriam reached for her. Now she headed straight to Miriam's hands.

"Star is the right name for you, because you're pretty as a star," Miriam said. Settling onto a hay bale, she cuddled the kitten on her lap and leaned in to hear her whispery purrs.

"That's a stupid name. Stars ain't pretty. They're just lights in the sky."

Miriam leapt up. The kitten wriggled out of her hands.

"Who said that?" she demanded, even though she knew. Hurrying back to the trough, she tipped her head back and looked into the space that only moments ago had been empty.

There, peering down at her, were the same brown eyes she had seen when she was here with Zayde. The eyes looked curious, but not exactly friendly.

Did they belong to a boy or a girl? Whoever it was hadn't spoken long enough for Miriam to tell. But boys didn't use words like *pretty*. It had to be a girl. A girl!

"Who are you?" Miriam asked.

"I'm me," came the answer.

"What kind of name is that?"

"It ain't my name." Whoever she was, she sounded impatient. Maybe even angry. Miriam wondered how old she was and wished she could see all of her face, not just her eyes. "I'm not telling you my name," the girl added.

"Why not?" Miriam asked.

"I shouldn't even be talkin' to you."

"Then why are you?" Miriam snapped back before she could stop herself. Where had that boldness come from? She had never talked to anyone in that kind of voice before. It felt good!

The girl did not reply. Miriam's neck was beginning to hurt. She glanced down at the hay bale. If she could lie down on it, she wouldn't have to keep standing like this, with her head tipped back.

Something touched her boot. She jumped, expecting to see the girl standing right beside her. But it was only Star brushing up against her. Miriam had been so caught up with the girl in the loft that she had forgotten about the kittens. She crouched down and cradled Star. By the time she turned back to the loft, the eyes were gone.

"Where are you?" she asked.

There was no answer.

"Where did you go?"

Still nothing.

Miriam put Star back on the floor with the rest of the kittens. If the girl wasn't going to show her face, Miriam would find her herself. Never mind that Zayde had said a hayloft wasn't a place for a girl. Clearly it was.

NINE

The easiest way to get into the hayloft was to climb the wide wooden staircase outside the barn. The men used it in the fall to get the hay inside. The staircase was visible from the corner of the farm where they were building the new barn. It was also visible from the window in the farmhouse kitchen. Bubby often looked out the window while she worked.

The best way for Miriam to get into the hayloft without anyone seeing was to use the inside ladder. It was nailed to the wall near the room with the woodstove. She had watched some of the men use it. They scrambled up the rungs as gracefully as the kittens jumped onto hay bales. They made it look easy.

Now, standing before the ladder, Miriam realized it wasn't going to be easy at all. She placed her hands on the rung that was level with her shoulders. Because the ladder was nailed to the wall, it was impossible to get a good grip. There was nowhere for her hands to go—she couldn't hold on to the rungs the way she would a normal ladder.

She reached for the side rails. Pressing her knuckles against the wall and her thumbs on the rails, she lifted her right foot onto the bottom rung. Then she pulled up her left foot and slowly began climbing, willing her feet to be steady. It was a challenge, balancing on such a small space. And her feet weren't even that big. How did the men manage? Flattening her hands and clenching them into fists again, she inched closer to the loft opening. If only she could hold on to the rungs, the trip would go so much more quickly. But the higher she climbed, the more it became apparent that even if she had managed a secure hold, the trip would not have been smooth. As she pressed her hands against the rail sides, she could feel slivers digging into her fingers.

Keep climbing, she told herself. Don't think about the slivers. Think about how brave Esther was. Do what you have to do.

She kept her eyes focused on the wall in front of her. She wondered if the girl was watching her. But the one time she looked up, she saw nothing except the opening to the loft, and she nearly lost her balance, so it wasn't a very long look. Steadying herself led to more slivers. She wondered if the girl got slivers when she climbed the ladder. When Miriam got slivers back home, her mother removed them with a needle. How did the girl get rid of her slivers? Was there someone up there to take care of her? She was picturing the scene, a girl and her mother, a needle in a hayloft, when she heard the barn door open.

She looked toward the door and then down toward the floor. That's when she realized that instead of being almost to the top of the ladder like she thought, she had barely moved. She was only three rungs off the floor! She jumped down and ran as quickly as she could back to the stall with the kittens.

Safely hidden, she peeked through a tiny opening in the swinging doors. There was Joe, walking swiftly toward the back of the barn. Had he seen her attempting to climb up? He went straight to the ladder and took the rungs two at a time. He practically flew up into the loft.

It wasn't unusual for the hired men to visit the barn in the middle of the afternoon. But why was Joe in such a hurry? And why was it so easy for him and so hard for Miriam to climb the ladder? She quietly closed the stall doors and hurried toward the trough, hoping to hear through the opening whatever conversation might take place up there. It was obvious Joe wasn't there for hay. He was talking in an impatient whisper.

"Where are you?"

Miriam almost opened her mouth to answer. Then she realized Joe couldn't be talking to her— he hadn't even seen her. She got down on the floor and slid under the trough, in case he peered through the opening. The splinters in her hands stung.

She brought one hand to her mouth and tried to remove the little pieces of wood with her teeth.

Moses came over and started licking Miriam's face with his sandpaper tongue just as she pulled out another splinter. Pirate and Bandit put their front paws on her boots. She tried not to giggle as she listened for more sounds from the hayloft.

"Cissy!" Joe whispered. He sounded mad.

Cissy? So the brown-eyed girl's name was Cissy. But why was Joe looking for her?

"Shhhhh!" The voice didn't sound anything like the girl who had spoken to Miriam. This person sounded worried—or even scared. For a moment Miriam thought maybe a second person was hiding up there. But that couldn't be. Joe had only called out one name. More likely, Cissy, the same person who had been so self-assured and almost mean to Miriam, was as afraid of Joe as Miriam had been of her. Miriam wished the kittens would stop moving. Their rustling in the hay was making it hard to hear anything.

After the *Shhhhh!* Miriam didn't hear another word. The hayloft was big, covering the entire barn.

Cissy would have seen Miriam running to the stall. So she and Joe had taken their argument—Miriam was sure it was an argument—as far from the stall as possible. But what were they arguing about? And who was Cissy? How did Joe know her?

TEN

At dinner that night, Miriam sat where she always did, between Bubby and Banjo, across the table from Joe. Since that first day at lunch, she hadn't paid much attention to him at mealtimes. He did eat a lot, but all of the men did. Bubby said they needed to fill themselves up because they worked so hard.

Tonight Miriam couldn't take her eyes off Joe. And he noticed. He stared right back, not in a mean way, but not exactly friendly either. He didn't want to be observed. Miriam turned her gaze to the meat and carrots and beets on her plate, then lifted her eyes so he couldn't tell that she was still watching. That's when she saw him dropping food into his lap.

At first she thought she was imagining it, but the second time a hunk of Bubby's brown bread slid off Joe's plate and disappeared and he failed to reach down to retrieve it, she remembered that first lunch at the farm. Now she understood. He was taking food for Cissy. And he knew Miriam was still watching, because after that second piece of bread disappeared, he didn't take another morsel of food. Cissy wasn't going to get much to eat tonight, and it was Miriam's fault. She wished she could let Joe know that his secret was safe with her, that he could take as much food as he needed and she wouldn't say a word. But right now that sort of communication was not possible.

What *was* possible, she realized later that night as she got ready to recite her prayers, was Miriam helping to feed Cissy. "God bless Mama, Papa, Uncle Avram, Rafael, Gabriel, Anna, Ida, Bubby, Zayde and all my other family and friends," she said as her grandmother listened at the edge of the bed. "Keep them safe and healthy, and bring

Mama and Papa and Uncle Avram and my baby cousins back home very soon."

"Good night, Miri," Bubby said, giving her a kiss. Then she turned off the light, leaving Miriam to devise a plan.

⤚

The next afternoon, with a chunk of cheese in one coat pocket and the last two hamantaschen wrapped in a handkerchief in the other, Miriam hurried to the barn. More elaborate meals would have to wait until she could find a proper container and had mastered the ladder. Until then she needed both hands. She was sure she could climb the ladder now—she had practiced it in her head so many times before falling asleep, she was surprised she hadn't dreamed about it.

All she had to do was press the toes of her boots against the wall and grip the side rails with her fingertips. The trick would be to catch Cissy by surprise. That required entering the barn in silence. Miriam was huffing and puffing like a train about to sound its whistle. She stood in the cold trying to catch her breath and praying that the door wouldn't stick as it often did. When that happened, it made a horrible noise.

"Please be quiet today," she whispered as she reached for the wooden handle. Gritting her teeth, she slid the door open just enough to slip in sideways. Then she tugged it gently closed, hoping it wouldn't squeak or groan. Her wish came true. The door didn't make so much as a *whoosh*.

When she reached the ladder, she stopped and studied it. How could it possibly have gotten so much longer overnight? And had the rungs been that narrow yesterday? She was certain that wasn't possible.

"Don't be scared."

That's what she was saying in her head. *Don't be scared.* But the words sounded like they were outside her head.

She heard a voice again.

"What are you so scared about?"

Miriam shook her head, then tapped each side. It wasn't until she heard the giggling that she realized the words weren't actually coming from her.

"What you doing?" she heard Cissy ask, the end of the sentence lost in laughter.

She couldn't believe how friendly Cissy sounded. She'd changed overnight, just like the ladder. Her voice was so much warmer than it had been when she'd peered down from the hayloft.

Miriam realized the voice wasn't coming from the hayloft. Cissy wasn't talking to her. She was talking to the kittens!

"You stop pesterin' your mama like that," she continued. "You keep doing that and she ain't going to feed you no more."

Miriam backed away from the ladder. Slowly, stealthily as a tiger, she tiptoed toward the stall and the sound of Cissy's voice.

"Stop that!" Cissy was laughing louder now, a cross between a hiccup and a gulp. "You're tickling me!"

Which kitten was she talking to?

Miriam heard a little thump and then mewing.

"You're all right," Cissy said. "Don't you be fussin'. You're just fine."

Miriam wondered what had happened.

"I'm going to take care of you, don't you worry. Oooh! You stop that! Stop tickling me!" She laughed again, the hiccup and gulp.

Miriam put her hand to her mouth to stop herself from joining in. She was curious about the way Cissy talked. Papa and Zayde chopped off their words, sometimes at the beginning, sometimes at the end. But Cissy's words slid off, softly, almost like a melody. Miriam liked it. Part of her wanted to remain out here all afternoon, pressed up against the wall, eavesdropping. If she walked in, Cissy might run away or, worse, be as unfriendly as she had been the day before.

Miriam jammed her hands into her pockets. Her fingers brushed against the hamantaschen and cheese. If someone brought me food, she thought, I wouldn't be mean to them. The only way to find out if Cissy would be the same was to open the stall door.

ELEVEN

A black girl was sitting cross-legged on the floor, her back to the door. Her hair was short and fuzzy. It stuck out all over, like dandelion fluff, only darker. When she heard the door swing open, she bolted up and turned around so fast that Miriam jumped back and the kittens scattered.

"What are you doing here?" the girl demanded.

Seeing all of Cissy, not just her eyes, shocked Miriam into silence. She had never seen anyone so skinny in her entire life.

Cissy was only slightly taller than Miriam, but she was no wider than a broom handle. She wore thick wool stockings and a plaid dress—if you could call it a dress. Miriam was positive it was a shirt that was clearly intended for someone far bigger. The sleeves were rolled up so many times it looked as if Cissy wore donuts on each wrist. Her boots didn't appear to fit any better—there was no way anyone as short and skinny as Cissy was could have feet that big. The boots probably weighed more than she did.

"Ain't you supposed to be making cheese with your granny?" Cissy demanded, not taking her eyes off Miriam. "That's what your grandpa said. I heard him. What are you doing back here? Don't you dare tell anyone you saw me."

She began moving toward the door. Miriam, who was closer, backed up and blocked it. Cissy looked her up and down.

"What are you doing?" She was more confused now than angry. "Get out of my way."

Miriam shook her head, the words *be brave, be brave* swimming in her brain. She reached into her pockets again. Now did not seem like a good time to offer up cheese and cookies.

"I have to go! Your granny's going to come here lookin' for you. She'll find me and—just get out of my way! Don't make me push you."

"Nobody's coming," Miriam said firmly. She was surprised at how bossy she sounded. But it worked. Cissy stepped back as if *she'd* been pushed. "It's just me. Bubby's making cheese, like you said, but by herself. So be quiet! If someone does come, you can hide. You could hide in the trough and nobody would see you."

"I ain't going in that trough. I ain't that skinny. I'd get stuck in there."

"I don't think so," Miriam said.

Cissy shook her head. "I *know* so."

"How do you know?" Miriam asked.

"'Cause I *did* get stuck in there, that's how," Cissy said, crossing her arms across her chest.

Miriam pictured Cissy trapped in the trough, unable to free herself, the kittens crawling around on top of her, licking her, scratching her, getting their claws tangled in her puff of hair. She covered her mouth, but it was too late. Out burst the laughter she'd been holding in since before she entered the stall. She started laughing so hard she was crying.

Cissy looked indignant. Her eyebrows scrunched, and Miriam wasn't sure if she was going to scold Miriam or snap at her.

But then, much to Miriam's surprise, Cissy began to laugh too. It started small but quickly grew to a whoop. The next thing Miriam knew, Cissy was crouched over, hugging her knees and trembling. Miriam had never seen anyone shake with laughter before and wondered if Cissy might actually be crying. Then Cissy tumbled head over heels onto the floor.

"Are you all right?" Miriam asked. "Are you hurt?"

Cissy turned her face toward Miriam. "Fine," she said between giggles. "I'm fine!"

Miriam pulled the food out of her pocket. "I brought this for you," she said, waving it in front of Cissy's face. "To eat."

Cissy sat up and took the food. "I wouldn't have thought you'd brought it for me to wear on my head." She unwrapped the package, inspecting the hankie before she paid any attention to the food."This is awful fancy," she said. "Too nice to use." She wiped her face on her arm. "That's what sleeves are for."

Miriam wiped her eyes on her own coat sleeve.

That started Cissy howling again. "Are you telling me you ain't got a hankie for your own nose? You're going to mess up that pretty coat? Your granny's going to whup you!"

"She won't whup me," Miriam said. "Nobody whups me!" She had never heard anyone say *whup* in her life, and it struck her as the funniest word ever. "Whup, whup, whup," she said, until Cissy lay back on the floor, jammed her fingers in her ears and, between bursts of laughter, begged her to stop.

"I'm going to pee myself if you don't shut your mouth!" she pleaded.

Miriam was trying to remember the last time she had laughed so hard when Cissy, suddenly calm, sat up and looked at her with a satisfied smile.

"Your name is Miriam, right?"

Miriam nodded.

"I'm Cecilia, but everyone calls me Cissy. And I knew you were going to come in here and be my friend."

The announcement took Miriam by surprise. "No, you didn't."

"I did," Cissy insisted. "My mama told me."

Miriam looked around the stall. Her mama? So there *was* someone else here! "Your mama is here?" she asked.

Cissy shook her head. Her voice turned serious. "My mama's dead. But I talk to her every day and every night. And she told me I should be nice to you."

Miriam was confused.

"You *can* talk to dead people," Cissy assured her.

Talking to dead people wasn't what Miriam was confused about. That hadn't even occurred to her. "You *weren't* nice to me," she said.

"What do you mean?" Cissy said. "I only just met you."

"In the barn yesterday, when you were in the hayloft and you said Star was a stupid name. That wasn't nice."

Cissy looked at her lap. She rubbed her hands together as if washing them. "Sorry," she said finally. "I was just—well, I was—scared."

"Of me?" As far as Miriam knew, no one had ever been afraid of her before.

Cissy nodded. "Nobody's supposed to know I'm here. You can't tell anybody!"

"I won't!" Miriam assured her. She didn't have anyone to tell—except for Bubby and Zayde. She didn't think they would tell anyone either. But they probably wouldn't want someone sleeping in the hayloft. Especially not a girl.

"If we're going to be friends, you have to promise you ain't going to breathe a word about me. Not to nobody." Cissy slid her palm from her chin up over her lips, as if she were sealing her mouth closed. "Joe says if anybody finds out I'm here, I'll be sent to an orphanage."

"An orphanage?" Miriam asked.

"For children that ain't got no folks," Cissy explained.

"I know what an orphanage is," Miriam said.

"But what does Joe have to do with it? How do you even know him?"

"He's my brother," Cissy replied.

As soon as Cissy spoke, Miriam realized she should have figured that herself. Joe's brown eyes crinkled up just like Cissy's when he laughed. "That's why he takes the food for you."

"'Course he does," Cissy said. "If it weren't for him, I'd be starved half to death."

Miriam thought Cissy looked starved half to death anyway, but she didn't say so. "So are you an orphan? Or a hobo? I thought only men could be hobos."

Cissy's eyes widened. "We ain't hobos. What makes you think that kind of nonsense?"

"Didn't you come here on the train?" Miriam asked.

"Just because you come on the train, it doesn't mean you're a hobo," Cissy said. "Did *you* ride the train here?"

Miriam nodded.

"Are *you* a hobo?"

Miriam shook her head.

"Then there you go."

"But you're an orphan?" Miriam had never met an orphan before.

Cissy nodded. "An orphan. But not a hobo."

TWELVE

Cissy and Joe were from Mississippi. Joe was fifteen, only four years older than Cissy, but he looked older. That made it easier for him to find work. Joe and Cissy used to have two other brothers, Levi and Benjamin. They had died in the same fire that killed their parents.

Cissy told the story in a matter-of-fact voice, as if she were reciting words for a spelling bee. She and Miriam were sitting cross-legged on a hay bale, Cissy eating cheese, and Miriam cradling Star.

"After they died," Cissy went on, "we had to live with my mama's brother, Uncle Hesh, because he's the only relative we knew. His wife is Auntie May.

Uncle Hesh was horrible, and his wife wasn't much better. Meaner than fifteen cats in a bag, both of them. Auntie May told me I didn't need any more schooling, so I had to help her clean houses for all the rich folks in town."

"No school ever?" That didn't sound so bad to Miriam. Although she did like learning new things. But then she realized that Cissy might not even know how to read. She was afraid to ask.

"I had school before that, and I'm going to go again someday," Cissy said. "I even got some books here, for sums and reading and such. Joe got them for me. He got to go to school sometimes, but mostly Uncle Hesh dragged him all around the county to build houses with him, hammering and nailing and pounding and all that. Joe was so dog-tired he couldn't hardly keep his eyes open. And he doesn't want to be no housebuilder anyhow. One night he tells me we're leaving. We're going to find the better uncle, the one that came up north before I was born."

Miriam didn't understand. "If your uncle lives here, why aren't you staying in his house?"

Cissy shook her head. "We don't know exactly where he lives. Someplace in New York. Joe's going to find him, and then we can go live with him."

"What if he's meaner than fifteen cats in a bag?" Miriam asked.

"He ain't," Cissy said with a smile. "Uncle Hesh and Auntie May call him a half-witted hound. Everybody else they say that about I think is nice. So he probably is too. We just have to find him."

"How?" Miriam asked. Her parents were traveling halfway across the world, but at least they knew where they were going and who they were looking for. Cissy didn't even know her New York uncle's last name.

"Joe's got a plan," Cissy said. She seemed so convinced that Miriam felt it would be rude to keep asking questions.

"What made you and Joe stop here?" she asked.

"'Cause the train passes by," Cissy explained. "And your grandparents' house got a mark."

"What kind of mark?" Miriam asked.

"The hobo mark." Cissy paused to eat more cheese. "This is good. Your granny make it?"

Miriam shook her head. "We bought it at the market. She only makes soft cheese. What's a hobo mark?"

"It's like a secret code," Cissy said. "Only hobos know it."

"But you're not a hobo," Miriam reminded her.

Cissy shrugged. "You get to know stuff when you ride the trains. You get to talking to people, and you learn what you need to know. Like about how some houses got good marks and others got bad ones."

"Where's the mark on Bubby and Zayde's house?"

"Whose house?"

"Bubby and Zayde," Miriam repeated. "My grandparents."

"Them's their names?" Cissy asked.

Miriam shook her head. "That's what Jewish people call their grandparents. *Bubby* means 'grandmother' and *Zayde* means 'grandfather.'"

"Where you come from?"

"Brooklyn," Miriam said. "That's in New York. But where's the mark?"

"I can't tell you that," Cissy said.

"Why not?" Miriam asked.

"'Cause it's like a secret code. Just for hobos."

"You just said you're not a hobo."

"It doesn't matter," Cissy said. "You gotta respect the code. All I can tell you is that the mark on your grandpa's house says nice people live there and they'll give you a job and food."

Cissy finished off the cheese and then turned her attention to the pastries. Holding one up to her nose, she sniffed loudly and made a face. "I never ate nothing shaped like this before. What is it?"

"It's hamantaschen," Miriam explained. "It means 'Haman's pocket.' Although some people call it 'Haman's hat.' So you *could* wear it on your head, I guess. But I wouldn't recommend it!"

"That's a funny name. Who's Haman? And how come I'm eating his pocket? Or his hat?"

Miriam laughed. "He was a villain—thousands of years ago. He wanted to kill all the Jews." She had never had to describe what Purim was all about. Back home, everyone she knew had always celebrated the holiday. She paused for a moment to figure out how to tell it best.

"Haman is a character in a story, the book of Esther," she went on. "Esther was an orphan. Like you! She had a cousin, Mordecai, who found out about Haman's evil plan. Mordecai told Esther, and Esther went to the king and told on Haman. The king punished him. And now we celebrate this holiday, Purim. One of the things we do is tell the story, so we never forget, and another is to eat hamantaschen."

Cissy was doubtful. "She just went to the king? And he listened, just like that?"

"She was married to him," Miriam said.

"Well, maybe you should have mentioned that! And how come the cookie's not named after her or that Morty guy? Why'd you name a cookie after someone who wanted to kill people? That's about the craziest thing I ever heard."

"I guess I never thought about it that way," Miriam said.

"And whose holiday is it? I ain't never heard of no holiday called—what'd you call it?"

"Purim. It's a Jewish holiday," Miriam said. "I'm Jewish."

Cissy regarded Miriam curiously. "I ain't never met no Jewish person before."

"And I've never met anyone hiding in a barn before," Miriam said.

"I guess we're even then," Cissy said. She looked at the cookie again.

"Try it," Miriam said. "It's good. I promise."

Cissy took a deep breath. Then she bit off a tiny corner of the triangle and chewed it thoughtfully. A smile spread across her face. She took a larger bite.

"It is peculiar," she said. "But it ain't as bad as I feared." She studied the cookie, poking her finger into the opening in the middle. "What's this brown stuff here? It's like black sand or something, but sort of sweet."

"It's mohn," Miriam said.

"What?"

"Poppy seeds cooked with honey."

"So why don't you just call it poppy seeds cooked with honey?" Cissy said.

"I don't know," Miriam replied. "Probably because it takes too long to say that. Mohn is shorter.

That's its name. Poppy seeds and honey are just what it's made of. Why do we call bread *bread* instead of calling it yeast and flour and water and sugar and salt?"

"I guess I don't really care what it's called, as long as it tastes good," Cissy said, popping the entire second hamantaschen into her mouth.

THIRTEEN

Miriam didn't want to leave the barn. She had never met anyone like Cissy, and she had so many questions. She could have stayed for a week and not run out of things to ask or talk about. But Cissy knew better.

"If you don't get back to the house soon, your granny's going to get worried, and then she'll come out here, and that'll be the end of me." Moses, who was sitting on Cissy's lap, stood on his back legs and reached up to rest his front paws on her arm. "What are you doing, you silly cat?" She nudged him back down, then looked at Miriam again.

"She knows I'm just out here with the kittens," Miriam said. "She won't worry."

"But she might start getting suspicious. It's not good for me if she comes out here looking for you."

"Aren't you going to be lonely?" Miriam looked up toward the loft. "It's so cold. And dark. And how do you go to the bathroom?" She doubted that Cissy had a chamber pot. It didn't seem practical, let alone possible, to carry such an item up and down the ladder.

"Don't be worrying about me." Cissy stroked Moses, who had settled back into her lap. "I have been doing just fine. I got these kitties to keep me company. And all them cows. You cannot believe how loud cows get. It's like listening to a bunch of old folks snoring all night long. And Joe comes to see me." Cissy paused, looking a bit concerned. "But you're coming back tomorrow, right?"

Miriam nodded.

"Well, I'll see you then."

◦───◦

The sun had moved almost all the way to the west by the time Miriam slid the barn door closed behind her. She walked slowly back to the house.

The snow was beginning to melt. Slushy mud covered the path. But it wasn't just the mud that Miriam wanted to avoid. She was in no hurry to get back to the house and see Bubby. She didn't trust herself not to spill the beans about Cissy.

Up until now, the only secret Miriam had ever sworn to keep was Anna's surprise birthday party nearly one year earlier. She'd only had to stay quiet about it for two weeks, and she'd nearly ruined the whole thing when Anna started going on about how she and Charlie Chaplin had been born on the same day. Ida had kicked her so hard under the table that Miriam's ankle had been bruised for weeks. If she spilled the beans about Cissy, there would be a whole lot more trouble than a bruised ankle—or at least that's what Cissy seemed to think.

It felt wrong to keep Cissy a secret from Bubby and Zayde. Miriam was sure they would welcome her. They would probably even invite her to share Miriam's room. How wonderful would that be? Out in the barn, Cissy had made the possibility of the orphanage seem so real. Now, halfway to the house, Miriam wasn't so convinced that Cissy should keep hiding.

Through the kitchen window, she could see Bubby standing by the stove. She knew she should go inside and offer to help, but she was curious to see if she could find the mark that Cissy had mentioned.

Slowly she circled the house, scanning the walls and windows and shutters. The dimming light made it hard to see, but when she spotted a sprinkling of white splotches running down the side of the front-room window, her heart began to race. She had found the mark, she was sure of it! But when she got closer, she realized that what had looked like a sign drawn by a hobo was bird poop that had dribbled down the wall and dried there. She stared for a minute more, willing the poop to turn into a message, but her eyes got blurry and her feet were wet. It was time to go inside.

Bubby must have seen her. She was on the porch waiting, patting her hands on her apron. "What are you doing out there? Did you lose something?"

Miriam shook her head. "I was just looking for—" She stopped. How could she tell her grandmother what she had been doing without giving Cissy away?

"Did your grandfather tell you that story about the hobo mark?" Bubby asked. She shook her head, more amused than angry. "He does go on about that. I'm surprised he wasn't out there with you."

Miriam nodded, feeling her face grow hot. She did not like to be untruthful, but she had made a promise. Even if she thought it was unnecessary, a promise was a promise. "Do you know where the mark is?"

Bubby shook her head. "There is no mark. It's just a story the men cooked up to entertain each other. Your zayde likes a good story, but I know every inch of this house, inside and out. If there was a mark, I'd have seen it."

Bubby sounded as certain as Cissy had been. Who was right? Miriam didn't have time to think about it anymore, because Bubby was holding the door, shooing her inside.

～⌀

The next morning Miriam could not concentrate on her lessons. Her mind kept wandering back to the barn. When Bubby suggested she get started on her weekly letter to Mama and Papa, the thing she wanted to write about was Cissy. But instead she described her search for the hobo mark and told her parents that Bubby was looking forward to making a trip to Utica to purchase Passover supplies. Thinking of all the preparation made Miriam homesick. Back in Brooklyn, every store in the neighborhood stocked up for Passover. You didn't have to travel more than a block to find matzah and potato starch and horseradish.

She stared down at the notepaper, doing her best to think of something else cheerful that wouldn't require her to break her promise to Cissy. *The kittens are getting bigger,* she wrote. *Now I go to the barn by myself to play with them, and it's quite fun. They are very good company.* That was true, even if it wasn't the whole story.

FOURTEEN

Miriam hurried out to the barn after lunch, meatloaf in one coat pocket, roasted parsnips in the other. Both were wrapped in waxed paper, as much to protect her pockets as the food. The last thing she wanted on laundry day was to have to concoct a story for Bubby about why her clothes were stained.

She pushed at the wooden latch and slid the door open. As she closed the door behind her she heard Cissy's voice.

"Hey! Up here!"

She turned on the light. Up in the loft, she could see an arm hanging from the opening, waving an invitation.

"Come on up! The kitties and me are having a party."

Miriam skipped to the bottom of the ladder, then stopped abruptly.

Cissy was resting on her stomach, her face peering out of the opening, both hands dangling down now. For a second Miriam thought maybe Cissy could just pull her right up. But Cissy offered only a question. "What you waiting for?"

Miriam attempted a smile. Then she placed her hands on the railings and brought her right foot to the bottom rung. "Be brave," she whispered, her own voice drowning out the ones in her head that were saying there was no way she could climb to the top.

She looked up at Cissy again, who didn't seem to notice that she was trembling. "The kitties say they want to dance with you," Cissy said eagerly. "A waltz, or maybe a jig."

Still gripping the ladder rails, Miriam willed her left foot onto the rung.

"Wait a second," Cissy said. "Step back." Cissy scrambled up off the hayloft floor and was suddenly sliding down the ladder like a sled down a hill. Miriam watched, her mouth open. Could she ever be that graceful? That strong? She was still working on brave, and that was enough of a challenge.

"You've never done this," Cissy said. She smacked herself in the forehead with the palm of her hand. "I plumb forgot about that day. You thought you were so good, and you barely got off the ground."

A flush of heat spread across Miriam's cheeks.

"It's all right," Cissy assured her. "I was kind of praying you wouldn't come up. I think that's why you couldn't, you know. Sometimes thinking something's as powerful as doing something."

Miriam wasn't sure if this was the most sensible thing she had ever heard or the silliest.

Cissy continued. She sounded a bit like a schoolteacher. "Mind's the most powerful thing there is. That's what my mama used to say."

Miriam shook her head. She wanted to tell Cissy that the real reason she hadn't been able to get up the ladder was she was scared. But maybe

Cissy was right. *Thinking something's as powerful as doing something.* The truth was, Miriam didn't want to be scared anymore. She just wanted to climb that ladder, and she wanted to do it with grace and confidence.

"I'll be right behind you," Cissy said. "That way if you start to fall, you don't have to worry, 'cause I got your back. And your feet too."

All the way up, Cissy encouraged Miriam. "Hold on a little tighter there, like that. That's right."

"It hurts!" Miriam said as a fresh sliver dug into her palm. "How do you do this every day?"

"It don't hurt, really. You're just not accustomed to it is all. Couple more times up and down and you won't even think about it. It's like you blink your eyes and just like that, you're there. I promise."

Miriam wanted to believe Cissy was right, but it was hard to muster confidence when her arms were burning and her legs shaking. If she lost her balance, she would knock Cissy right off the ladder. She wasn't sure she could keep climbing.

"Go on," Cissy urged.

"Maybe I should go back down and try again after I rest," Miriam suggested.

"You're already halfway up," Cissy said. "Why would you go back down just to have to climb up all over again? You want to hang there another minute, that's fine by me. But you ain't going back down until you get all the way up."

Finally, balanced on the third rung from the top, Miriam found herself staring into the expanse of the loft.

"There you go!" Cissy's voice was triumphant. "You did it! Now you just climb up that last bit and flop onto your tummy and scooch. Go on." Cissy laid a gentle hand on the back of Miriam's legs, just above her knees. "Up and over. Just like that."

Miriam climbed the last rung and did as Cissy said. As she flopped onto the hay-covered floor, she started to giggle. "I feel like a snake. And I'm getting hay all over me."

"Don't you worry about that," Cissy said. "It comes off." She pushed at the bottom of Miriam's boots, urging her forward. "Now get out of the way already and make some room for me."

FIFTEEN

Miriam pushed herself to her knees and took in her surroundings. Hay bales were stacked like enormous bricks, from the floor to the slanted rafters of the ceiling. Somewhere up here were windows—she had seen them from outside the barn, and they were clearly the source of what little light there was—but for now all she could see was hay.

She turned to Cissy. "Where do you sleep?"

Cissy pointed to the opposite end of the loft, toward the back of the barn.

"Is that over the stall where the kittens are?" Miriam asked.

Cissy nodded. "Joe sussed it out. He figured it was safest 'cause nobody ever goes to that end of the barn. Until you, that is."

"How do you even get over there?" Miriam didn't see any path.

"I got my ways," Cissy said. "Every couple of days I make a new route. I can't just have one path that I use all the time. Can't afford to have anybody get suspicious. The men come up here a lot, you know."

Miriam was picking hay off her coat and dropping it onto the floor. But every time she removed some, more seemed to take its place. "Will you show me?"

"Not if you keep cleaning yourself like that I won't," Cissy said.

Her sharp tone took Miriam by surprise. "I thought we were friends."

"We are," Cissy said. "But if you're so worried about getting hay on that coat of yours, you ain't going to want to be poking around up here. And that's what you gotta do if you want to see where I live."

Miriam jammed her hands into her pockets. "I'll stop!" she said. "And here." She handed Cissy the parcels she'd forgotten about.

"What's this?" Cissy asked.

"Lunch. Meatloaf and roasted parsnips."

Cissy's face softened. "That's awful nice of you." When she went to open one, the other package tumbled out of her hands. Miriam reached out and caught it before it hit the floor. Cissy held out her hand to take it, but Miriam put it back into her pocket.

"I'll give it to you when we get to your—" Miriam thought for a moment. She had no idea what she was about to see, but it certainly wasn't an apartment, which was the only other place she had visited friends. "Your room?"

"Ain't much of a room," Cissy said, with a laugh that sounded more like a snort. She held the meatloaf up to her nose. "Smells good!" She broke off a piece and put it into her mouth. "This is the first I've eaten all day. Sometimes Joe gets too busy, or he can't sneak away, and I have to wait. It sure was nice of you to think of me."

The meatloaf was gone in seconds. Cissy wiped her hands on the waxed paper, then folded it neatly. She was about to place it in her shirt pocket when Miriam reached out.

"I'll take it," she said. "It will be easier for me to throw it away."

"Thank you," Cissy said. "Okay, let's go. You've waited long enough to see my quarters."

Cissy began moving hay bales out of the way, stacking them to create an opening barely big enough for one person to stand. "You go," she said, motioning for Miriam to move in front of her. She replaced the bales so it looked as if nothing had been moved. Then she squeezed ahead of Miriam.

"They ain't so close together as they look from the top of the ladder," she explained as she moved more bales. She continued repeating the process— move bales, motion for Miriam to move in front, replace the bales, squeeze past. Pretty soon Miriam had no idea which end of the barn was which, or where she was.

"How do you know where to go?" she asked.

Cissy had been working so hard that her face glistened with sweat. But instead of looking weary, she wore a mischievous grin. "Twine," she said.

"Twine?"

"Like string, but stronger." Cissy reached down and felt around underneath the bale she had just replaced. She pulled out a piece of thin brown cord and handed it to Miriam. "The men use it to tie the hay bales." She pointed, and Miriam noticed for the first time how the bales were held together. The twine was almost the same color as the hay, so it had been easy to miss.

Miriam handed the twine back to Cissy, who replaced it under the bale nearest to them.

"Do you know the story of the minotaur and the maze?"

Miriam shook her head.

"It's a myth," Cissy said as she continued working, Miriam following close behind. "My daddy knew loads of them. He was a good story-teller." Cissy's voice had grown quiet and sad. Miriam worried she might be about to cry. But then she took a deep breath and went on.

"The story is about a boy who got sent into a maze. He was called Theseus." She looked over her shoulder at Miriam. "Ain't that peculiar?"

"It is," Miriam agreed.

"Anyhow, a king sent Theseus into the maze, and he was going to get eaten by a monster. The king's daughter didn't want that to happen, so she snuck him a ball of twine to use as a clue to get out. Theseus killed the monster, and then he used the twine to find his way back out again. I figured if it worked for Theseus, it'd work for me."

She stopped, removed three more bales and motioned for Miriam to squeeze past her again. Miriam expected to see another stack of hay, so she was surprised to discover that they had reached their destination, a cramped, narrow clearing in the bales. The space was so small that when Miriam spread her arms to the sides, her fingers brushed against hay.

In the middle of the clearing, taking up nearly all the space on the floor, was a worn brown blanket. Beneath the blanket was a faded sheet, and beneath that, more hay that Cissy had shaped to resemble a mattress. It looked almost like a real bed. The blanket was dotted with holes, its edges ragged. A shirt stuffed with hay served as a pillow.

"That's Joe's shirt," Cissy said matter-of-factly when she noticed Miriam staring. "It's nice having something of him here. Makes it less lonely."

Miriam remembered the first morning she had woken up in the farmhouse, how sad she had felt being so far from home and unsure when she might see Mama and Papa again. That thought had made her roll over and cry into her pillow.

Thinking of that now made her feel ashamed. She had nothing to cry about, not compared to Cissy. But Cissy seemed to think it was perfectly reasonable, even normal, to live in a cold, dark barn, never knowing when her brother would come to bring her food. Miriam didn't see any reason for her to live like this, not when, just across the farm-yard, there was a warm house with an empty bed.

"You should come and live in the farmhouse with me," Miriam announced.

The smile disappeared from Cissy's face. Her voice turned hard. "I told you, I can't do that."

"But it's so cold here, and dark. And there's so much room in the farmhouse, and Bubby and Zayde are good people. You know that. You know about the mark."

Cissy shook her head so hard that bits of hay flew out of her hair. "I showed you where I live so you'd see I'm fine. I don't need nothing. Though I appreciate that food you brought me. I thank you for that. But I don't need you dragging me into the open. I just need you to be my friend. If you are going to be my friend, that means not telling about me. No one. You promised."

She reached out and took Miriam's hand. For someone so slight, she had an awfully strong grip.

SIXTEEN

Those first few weeks after Miriam and Cissy became best friends, Miriam was haunted at night by the fear that she might let the secret slip. In one dream, she forgot that she was hiding food in her lap during dinner. When she stood, it slid off her dress and spattered all over the floor.

In another, she and Cissy were laughing so hard in the hayloft that Cissy fell through the opening above the trough. Instead of landing in the stall, she wound up in the milking parlor, right next to the stool where Zayde sat as he milked Corky.

The week before Passover, Miriam had the strangest dream of all. When she opened the door for Elijah at the seder, Cissy was there, in a brand-new white dress and shiny patent-leather shoes.

"A brand-new dress and shoes?" Cissy said when Miriam described the dream to her. They sat cross-legged in the loft, playing with the kittens. "I ain't had a new dress in forever."

Cissy was wearing the same thing she wore every day, the plaid flannel shirt that had belonged to her father and the black wool stockings that Joe had purchased for her at a five-and-dime store north of Maryland and south of New York State.

Miriam looked down at her own dress. Mama had sewn it. She'd used thick, dark-green serge. "It matches your eyes," Mama had said.

"It's different for you," Cissy said, her voice softening. "You live in a house, so you should be dressing nicely. I live in a barn, and I ain't got a sewing machine, but you don't need no machine to turn a shirt into a dress. Just a little ingenuity."

"Engine-ooity?" Miriam asked.

"That was one of my mama's favorite words. It means cleverness. Pretty clever, turning a shirt into a dress, don't you think?"

Miriam had to admit that it was.

"Now who's this Elijah, and why were you opening the door for him anyway?" Cissy said, changing the subject. "Shouldn't he come when dinner starts? Is he always late?"

Miriam laughed. "He's not a real person," she said.

Cissy narrowed her eyes and drew back, confused. "You invite fake people to your dinner, and you think they are going to show up?"

"It's part of the seder. That's the name of the dinner we have on the first night of Passover. We open the door for Elijah and invite him in to drink a glass of wine. He's a prophet—Elijah the Prophet."

"*That* Elijah?" Cissy said, as if Elijah were a friend she'd bumped into the day before. "From the Bible?"

"You know who Elijah is?" Now it was Miriam's turn to be confused.

"'Course I do," Cissy replied, and then she began to sing.

Satan is a liar and a conjurer too.

If you don't watch out, he'll conjure you.
If I could, I surely would
Stand on the rock where Moses stood.
Elijah Rock, shout, shout,
Elijah Rock, comin' up Lord.

The melody was sad and hopeful at the same time. But what was most surprising was Cissy's voice. Miriam couldn't believe something so powerful was coming out of someone who looked as if a strong wind could pick her up and blow her clear across a pasture.

Abruptly Cissy stopped singing. "What are you starin' at?" she asked Miriam. "You think I don't study the Good Book? I went to church, you know. Before I had to start hiding in here, I mean."

"Your voice," Miriam said, barely getting the words out. "It's beautiful."

Cissy shrugged, but she looked pleased. "Ain't nothing special."

"It sure sounds special to me," Miriam said.

Cissy pretended to bow. "Well, thank you, ma'am," she said. "I shall give you a front-row seat at my first concert."

"Where'd you learn that song?" Miriam asked.

"Church, I guess," Cissy replied. "Don't you go to church?"

Miriam shook her head. "Jewish people don't go to church. We go to synagogue."

"That like a church?"

"I don't know," Miriam replied. "I've never been to church. What do you do there?"

"Sing. Pray. Read scripture."

"Scripture?"

"The Bible." Cissy sounded impatient. "God's word."

"We read the Torah," Miriam said. "It's in Hebrew. But it's God's word too. So I guess it's kind of the same. But Elijah is Jewish, so why do you sing about him?"

"'Cause he's in the Good Book," Cissy said. "I told you. Now, I don't know what religion he is, but I don't think he's going to be coming to your house for dinner. He's been dead forever."

The way she said it made Miriam feel like a simpleton. For a moment she was mad at Cissy. She thought about stomping out of the barn and never coming back. Or, worse, threatening to spill the beans.

Cissy could tell. "I mean, everybody's got a right to believe what they want. Heck, my mama's dead, and I talk to her. It ain't up to me to be tellin' you what's wrong and right. But I still don't get why you'd invite someone to dinner and then just give him a drink when there's a whole meal in front of everybody else. 'Specially a dead someone."

"It's not really inviting," Miriam said, although now she was getting confused too. No one had ever challenged her to think about Elijah this way before. "It's what we do—we open the door for him. And only once a year, at the seder. *Seder* means 'order' in Hebrew. At the dinner, everything happens in a special order, and we do all kinds of things that we don't on other nights." Miriam thought maybe she was talking too much, but Cissy looked interested.

"Now tell me what else you do, besides inviting this Elijah in for a drink," Cissy said, putting on her serious, I'm-ready-to-learn voice.

"We don't eat bread, we eat—" Miriam was about to say *matzah* when Cissy suddenly put her index finger to her mouth and began shaking her head. Miriam heard what had made Cissy so worried—the unmistakable thud of footsteps.

The girls had often heard the men coming and going on the main floor of the barn, and Cissy would always hide under the trough. No one ever came into the stall when they were playing, but Cissy would not take any chances. Never, though, in the times they had been in the loft, had they heard footsteps so close.

Cissy leaned up against Miriam and put her mouth to her ear. When she began to whisper, her voice was reassuring. "He won't be here long." Her breath tickled Miriam's ear. "They never are, but usually they come in the morning, before you do. They must have needed more hay or something. Soon as we hear the barn door close, you've got to get out. I don't think they'll come back, but you never do know."

SEVENTEEN

Miriam slowly made her way back to the house. What would have happened, she wondered, if whoever had been up in the loft had stumbled upon her and Cissy? Not that any of the hired men were likely to find them. But there was always a danger that Joe might decide to surprise his sister. Miriam wasn't sure if she could hide fast enough if that happened. And if Joe discovered that Cissy and Miriam had become friends, he might decide that the farm was no longer safe. Then he would pack up Cissy and take her away. Cissy had said as much.

Having a friend to spend time with was so much better than having only kittens, but having a friend she couldn't tell anybody about—that was the hardest thing ever.

Bubby was waiting in the front hall. "You're looking gloomy," she said. "I've got news that will cheer you up." She handed Miriam an envelope. Miriam recognized Mama's handwriting immediately. "Your uncle and the babies are healthy enough to come to America. They should be home in just about a month!"

Miriam's eyes widened as she sat down at the kitchen table and unfolded three pieces of heavy white notepaper. "It's a long letter!" she said.

"It's not all words," Bubby said, but Miriam had already discovered that only the first piece of paper was a letter. The other two were pictures, drawn in precise, confident pencil strokes.

One showed two babies sleeping shoulder to shoulder in a crib. Both had dark, curly hair and pudgy hands and feet. Even though they were asleep, or perhaps because of it, their faces looked peaceful and sweet. In the other picture, they didn't look quite so peaceful. The artist had captioned the picture *Rifke and Gabriel and Zvi and Rafael.*

Mama was holding Gabriel. His eyes were bright and cheerful, and his mouth was wide open. Papa was holding Rafael, whose face was wrinkled into an expression between angry and sad. The picture was so lifelike that Miriam half expected to hear Gabriel laughing and Rafael wailing.

"Who drew these?" she asked.

"Your uncle Avram," Bubby answered, pointing to the sentence in the letter where Mama had described the "portrait sessions," as she called them.

"I thought he was a shopkeeper," Miriam said.

Bubby nodded. "That's how he earns a living," she said. "But he's an artist too."

"Can I keep them in my room?" Miriam asked. She was already looking forward to taking the pictures to the barn to show Cissy.

"If you'd like," Bubby said. "But let's wait until after dinner. I think your zayde would like to see them first."

Miriam ran her fingers over the picture of her parents and the twins. This was the first time she had really considered what it would mean to share her home with two babies. She did not know any babies.

Her other cousins were the same age as she was, or older.

"Do you think they will cry a lot?" she asked Bubby.

Bubby looked at the pictures again before she answered. "Babies do cry," she said finally. "But mostly because they can't use words. When they learn to talk, they don't cry as much. And sometimes if they're crying, all you have to do is hold them close and give them comfort, and they'll stop."

Miriam pointed to the picture of the crying Rafael. "That doesn't seem to be working for Papa," she said.

"I'm sure it will for you," Bubby said.

"I hope so," Miriam said. "They're going to be my brothers. They will be my cousins and my brothers."

Bubby nodded.

"Can we come here, to visit you?" Miriam said.

"You must and you should!" Bubby said. "I'm getting used to having a little girl around here.

I don't know what I'm going to do when you're gone. I certainly do hope you will come back and bring the twins."

"Will you be their bubby too?"

"Of course I will," Bubby said. "You bring them here, and we'll put them to work. You can teach them to milk a cow."

"I don't even know how to milk a cow," Miriam reminded her.

"Then we had better teach you soon," Bubby said.

~∽~

When Miriam went out to the barn the next day, Cissy shimmied down the ladder to greet her. "I think we'd best stay in the stall today," she said.

Miriam was worried. "Did anyone come into the loft after I left yesterday? Or this morning?"

"Just Joe," Cissy said. "But we haven't played down here in a while anyhow."

When they reached the stall, Miriam pushed open the door and stepped aside to let Cissy in first.

Moses came padding over. Cissy bent over and scooped him up. "Look how big he's getting," she said, holding him up in the air.

Miriam pulled Uncle Avram's pictures out from one pocket and two of Bubby's donuts from the other. As she plopped down on the hay-bale bench next to Cissy, she handed her the donuts Bubby had fried up early that morning. Miriam had rolled them in cinnamon sugar after Bubby removed them from the pan. They were light and fluffy and filling at the same time .

"These are for you," she said. "We had stew for lunch, so this is the best I could do."

Cissy's face brightened. "These the ones your granny made for breakfast?"

Miriam felt bad. "Joe brought you some too, didn't he?"

"Don't matter," Cissy replied, her mouth full. "Your granny makes the best donuts."

"I helped," Miriam said.

"Well, then you and your granny make the best donuts." Cissy swallowed and looked down at the papers in Miriam's hands. "Whatcha got there?"

"They're pictures," Miriam said.

Cissy finished the rest of the first donut. "You made donuts *and* pictures? You had a busy morning."

Miriam laughed. "Mama sent them. My uncle drew them." She unfolded the picture of the babies in their crib and held it up for Cissy to see.

"Those are your cousins?" Cissy asked, her voice full of wonder.

Miriam nodded. Cissy reached for the picture.

"Wipe your hands first, please," Miriam said, polite but firm. Cissy nodded and wiped her hands on her shirt. Then Miriam passed her the first picture so she could look more closely. Moses jumped off Cissy's lap, but she didn't seem to notice.

"What's the name of the place they live again?"

"Borisov."

"That is a right strange name."

"What's the name of the place you're from?" Miriam asked.

A smile broke out on Cissy's face. "Whiskey Corner," she said, laughing.

"Whiskey Corner? What kind of name is that for a town?"

"It isn't much of a town," Cissy said. "More like a collection of little shacks and houses. Long time ago it was the part of the county where people made whiskey, and when it turned into a town, nobody thought to give it a new name 'cause by then they all knew it as Whiskey Corner. So that's what it stayed." She returned the picture to Miriam. "What's the other picture?"

Miriam handed it to her, then folded up the first one and carefully placed it back into her pocket.

Cissy smoothed out the picture. "That's your mama and daddy?"

Miriam nodded.

Cissy chewed on her lip. Then she ran her fingers over the picture, just as Miriam had done. "I wish I had a picture of mine. Everything burned in the fire."

"I'm sorry," Miriam said.

"Ain't nothing you can do about it," she said. She looked up at Miriam, down at the picture and then back at Miriam. "Your mama's awful pretty. You look like her. And those babies, they have the same hair as you. They're going to look like you, I bet."

She studied the picture again. "That baby your daddy's holding—he doesn't look too happy. I hope he don't cry like that all the time when he comes to live with you."

"Me too!" Miriam said.

"When are they going to get here anyway?"

Miriam shrugged her shoulders. "Bubby thinks in a little more than a month. After Passover."

"That's that holiday with Elijah, the one you told me about yesterday?" Cissy patted the spot beside her. "Sit down already and tell me some more."

EIGHTEEN

"Did I tell you *why* we celebrate Passover?"

"So you can invite Elijah to dinner," Cissy said.

"That's only part of it," Miriam said. "A long time ago, the Israelites were slaves in Egypt. They had to build cities for the pharaoh. He was like the king."

"I know that," Cissy said.

"Because it's in the Bible?"

"And because there's songs about it. You know 'Go Down, Moses'?"

"No," Miriam said.

"Go down, Moses
Way down in Egypt land

Tell old Pharaoh to
Let my people go."

Today Cissy's voice sounded smoky and deep. It was strangely beautiful, and it sent shivers through Miriam.

"You cold or something?"

"Your voice," Miriam said. "I could listen to you all day long."

Cissy waved her hands. "I told you it ain't nothing special. Now keep talking. What do you eat on this holiday? Anybody's pockets?"

"We eat matzah," Miriam said.

"What's that?"

"It's like a giant cracker. Because when the Israelites left Egypt, they were in such a hurry they didn't have time to let their bread rise, so the bread wasn't big and soft, it was thin and crispy."

"Okay, so crackers. What else?"

"We also make little sandwiches."

"You eat sandwiches for dinner?"

Miriam shook her head. "The sandwiches are just for the first part of the seder. That's when we tell the story about how the Israelites escaped, and we talk about the special food we're supposed to eat."

"What kind of sandwiches?" Cissy asked, her eyes bright.

"Horseradish and *charoses*," Miriam said.

Cissy put her hand over her mouth. She looked horrified. Then, shaking her head, she said, "Horseradish? You're pulling my leg. That sounds awful! I'd rather stay in here and eat hay than sit at a table and eat horseradish."

"You only have to eat a little," Miriam said. "And then you get as much charoses as you want."

"Ha-roses?" Cissy asked.

"Charoses," Miriam said, making a growly sound in the back of her throat when she said the *ch*.

"What is that?" Cissy asked. She wrinkled her nose.

"It's good!" Miriam assured her. "Mama makes it. She chops up apples and nuts and mixes them with cinnamon and sugar and wine. It tastes almost like candy."

"Well, it does sound a lot better than horse-radish," Cissy said. "What else do you eat?"

"Chicken soup with matzah balls," Miriam said.

"I thought matzah was a cracker. It's a ball?"

"To make matzah balls you use matzah meal," Miriam explained. "It's like flour. And you mix it with eggs and water, so it's soft. Then you shape the dough into balls and boil them. When they're done you add them to the soup."

Cissy nodded. "Then what?"

"*Gefilte* fish. It's almost as good as charoses."

"Filtered fish?"

"Ge-FILT-uh fish," Miriam said.

"I heard of trout and rainbow fish, but what in the name of creation is a gefilte fish?"

Miriam giggled. "It's not just one fish," she said. "You mix different kinds of fish together. And then you add in onions and carrots, and you make it into balls, and—"

"You make everything into balls!" Cissy laughed. "Matzah balls. Fish balls. Do you eat baseballs? Don't you eat anything normal? Like, I don't know, grits? Or ham hocks?"

"What's grits?"

"It's sort of a corn mush," Cissy said. "My mama made the best grits. We'd eat them for breakfast, in a bowl, and sometimes, if we had sugar syrup, we'd put that on top."

A dreamy expression spread across Cissy's face. Miriam imagined Cissy must be remembering breakfast in Mississippi with her mama and papa.

"Okay, but isn't a hammock something you sit in?" Miriam asked.

"Not a *hammock*," Cissy said, laughing again. "Ham hocks. Bottom part of a pig leg. Mama stewed 'em with beans or greens. Best thing I ever ate. That and Hoppin' John."

"Hopping John?"

"Hoppin'," Cissy said. "No *g* at the end."

"Well, what in the name of creation is Hoppin' John?" Miriam asked. Her imitation made Cissy smile.

"Well," Cissy said seriously, sounding like a schoolteacher again, "Hoppin' John is something we eat on the special occasion of the new year. It is made with black-eyed peas and rice, and my mama made it with ham hocks 'cause that made it extra special. And you don't need to make any snorting noises to pronounce it neither. So there."

"What's a black-eyed pea?" Miriam asked. "I didn't even know peas *had* eyes." She was laughing now, right along with Cissy.

"It's special food—I don't think you have 'em up here. Least, nobody's ever brought me any from your granny's kitchen."

"No ham hocks either," Miriam said. "Ham isn't kosher."

"Kosher?"

"Jewish people don't eat any meat that comes from a pig," Miriam explained. "And we don't eat milk and meat together."

"So you have never had fatback? Or meatloaf with cheese melted on top?"

"Never. What's fatback?" To Miriam, the name made it sound very unappealing, but she didn't want to make Cissy feel bad by saying so.

"Kind of like bacon," Cissy said. The dreamy look came over her face again. "I sure do miss eating fatback."

"I wish I could make something you like," Miriam said.

"Don't you worry about that, Miri," Cissy assured her. "You've already done that."

Miriam didn't understand. None of the food she had brought for Cissy from Bubby's kitchen was anything she had asked for. And it was Bubby, not Miriam, who had made most of it. "How?" Miriam asked.

"You made me a friend."

NINETEEN

Every night before Miriam fell asleep, Bubby and Zayde came to her room and sat at the edge of her bed and listened as she recited the Sh'ma. The Sh'ma came from the Torah, and Miriam said it in Hebrew. After the Sh'ma, Miriam said a few more prayers, but these were in English, and they were her own words.

When she first arrived at the farm, Miriam used those prayers to give thanks for being blessed with a nice family and a warm place to sleep. She asked God to watch over those she loved, which included everyone from Mama and Papa to her cousins in Brooklyn and Borisov. Now, though, after Bubby and Zayde left her room she prayed that Cissy and Joe would find their uncle so that Cissy, too, would have a safe, warm place to live—but not until after Mama and Papa returned.

Miriam couldn't imagine life on the farm without Cissy. She didn't like to miss one day in the barn with her. The first time Bubby planned an activity that kept them in the house all day, Miriam spent almost the entire time worrying that Cissy would think she was never coming back. And indeed, the next day when Miriam came to the barn, Cissy confessed that she had been a little bit concerned.

"I kept hoping you'd come back," Cissy said. "But I've been through worse than losing a friend, you know. And you did come back! I bet you was more worried than me. I know you got your granny and grandpa in there to keep you busy. When you come out here, you come. When you don't, I know you will again."

One morning, the week before Passover, Bubby announced that there would be no lessons after breakfast. Miriam was so excited that her voice came out somewhere between a squeak and a shout. "I can go out to the barn right now?" she asked.

Bubby shook her head. "Miri, don't you remember? We're going to Utica today, to do our Passover shopping. I thought you were looking forward to a visit to the city. You can go back to the barn tomorrow. The kittens will survive one day without you."

A frown spread across Miriam's face before she could stop it. "I forgot," she admitted.

"And isn't it about time you decided which kitten you want to keep?" Bubby said. "Next week they will be eight weeks old. That's old enough to leave their mama. And then you won't have to go to the cold barn every day. Won't that be nice?"

No, Miriam thought, that will not be nice at all. "I like going to the barn," she replied, hoping she sounded less concerned than she was. "It's not that cold. And I don't know which kitten to pick yet."

Now Miriam felt ashamed. Two falsehoods in one sentence! The barn was always cold, and she was pretty sure which kitten she was going to keep.

"I know they're big enough," Miriam said. "But I don't want to take one away from all its brothers and sisters. It might be lonely." *And I'll be lonely too, and so will Cissy, if we don't get to visit each other every day.*

"I suppose so," Bubby said. "But cats can get used to lots of things. I don't think you need to concern yourself with that."

Zayde filled the truck with gasoline from the pump near the barn. Then he parked the truck in front of the house and boosted Miriam to sit in the middle of the front bench. Bubby climbed in, and soon they were on the road. Sometimes, when they went over a bump, Miriam's leg brushed against the long narrow gearshift sticking out of the floor.

They passed gentle rolling hills with farms whose fields were still covered with snow. Miriam wondered if there was as much mud on these fields as there was at Bubby and Zayde's. It was hard to tell from so far away.

The road that led into Utica was so long and steep that Miriam's ears popped all the way down. The streets in the city were much wider and more crowded than they were in Waterville. Zayde parked between the meat market and the grocery store. At the market, he started up a long conversation with the butcher, Sam. Miriam had seen Sam at the farm before. He came every few months to pick up a cow and bring it into his shop. The two men were still making plans for Sam's next visit when Bubby took Miriam by the hand and led her to the grocery store.

"What will Mama and Papa do for Passover?" Miriam asked as they entered the store. "Can you have Passover in the Old Country?"

"Of course you can," Bubby assured her. She picked up two baskets and handed one to Miriam. "Your mama and papa will have a seder with Uncle Avram's and Tante Chaya's family, may she rest in peace. And next year, you'll all be together in New York for the seder. Imagine that."

Miriam tried, but she was wondering what Mama and Papa's seder would be like this year.

How big would the table be? How many people would sit around it? Would Mama and Papa be able to find whitefish and pike for their gefilte fish? And did the stores in Borisov have the same kind of matzah as in America? She wondered if her parents missed her as much as she missed them right now.

"You're looking sad," Bubby said. She stopped in front of a display of matzah and began loading boxes into her basket and Miriam's. "I thought you liked Passover. Didn't you tell me it's your favorite holiday?"

Miriam nodded. She didn't want to upset Bubby, so she didn't tell her the truth, that Passover was her favorite holiday because having such a big family gathered together made the seder festive and fun. She had trouble believing that a seder at the farm would be festive at all.

"Why are you buying so much matzah?" she asked as Bubby put another box into her basket.

"Is this too heavy for you?" Bubby removed a couple of boxes.

"It's not that," Miriam said. "This seems like

a lot of matzah for just you and me and Zayde. We couldn't possibly eat all this in one week."

Nobody ate matzah after Passover. By the end of the one-week festival, everyone was so tired of it that they didn't want to look at it for another year. "Why do we need so much?" Miriam asked.

"What makes you think it's only for us?" Bubby asked.

"It's only you and me and Zayde at the seder," Miriam reminded her. "We're the only ones who celebrate Passover."

Bubby looked amused. "Where did that idea come from?" she asked.

"Who else could come?" There is nobody else, Miriam thought, but she couldn't think of how to say that without sounding unpleasant.

"The hired men, of course," Bubby said. "Where are they going to eat, if not with us?"

She gestured to Miriam to follow her to the next aisle.

"But they aren't Jewish," Miriam said. To keep up, she had to take two steps to Bubby's one. For an old lady, Bubby moved quickly.

"You don't have to be Jewish to come to a seder," Bubby said, now loading their baskets with walnuts for the charoses.

"But isn't it strange, having people who don't know anything about the holiday or why we do what we do? Won't they be bored?"

Bubby thought for a moment. "You'd have to ask them if they're bored," she said with a smile. "It's been so many years that we've had hired men around our seder table, I'm used to it." She paused again, longer this time. "I wouldn't say it's strange. But it does make me look at Passover differently. Sometimes, seeing things through other people's eyes helps you to understand things in a new way."

Miriam thought back to the conversations she'd had with Cissy about hamantaschen and Elijah's visit. She knew Bubby was right. But she didn't say so, for fear she'd let something slip. Instead, she nodded and followed her grandmother to the front of the store, where the clerk was waiting to ring up their purchases.

TWENTY

Dinner on the farm that night was lively, with the men talking about what they had done all day. Joe generally remained quiet, but he was actively joining in on the conversation. All of the men seemed determined to talk about what they had done, because Zayde had not been there to see for himself.

A new worker, Franklin, had arrived the previous week. He came from a dairy farm in Ohio. Nobody knew why he had moved on. The men weren't in the habit of talking about such things. Instead, he and Bart were discussing an underground railroad.

"We have underground railroads in New York," Miriam said, eager to join in the conversation. "We call them subways."

Franklin chuckled gently. "Ain't the same thing, miss," he said. "The Underground Railroad wasn't actually underground, and it stopped running before I was born." He paused. "Must have been around the 1870s. But Joe here was saying he had a great-great-uncle who traveled up north that way, and I had some relatives who told me there were stops around this part of New York. Right, Joe?" Franklin looked at Joe, who nodded.

"Why was it called underground if it wasn't underground?" Miriam asked.

"Not entirely sure," Franklin said. Miriam noticed that everyone had stopped talking to pay attention to him. "Some people say it's because it was hidden. It wasn't even an actual railroad. But we do know it was a way for slaves to escape from the south to the free states—Ohio, Pennsylvania, New York—and Canada. They escaped on foot, or sometimes on carts, and they had good people like you folk"—he looked over at Zayde—"helping them along the way. They called the stops 'stations.'"

Cissy hadn't said anything about what kind of train her uncle had taken to New York. However, Miriam knew enough to understand that if it was this underground one, a railroad that wasn't even a railroad and hadn't been in service for more than sixty years, it was going to be very hard to find out where he was. He might not even be alive.

Joe said as much. "I don't know where he went," he told Franklin. "It's almost like a legend, something we all talked about. Nobody heard from Uncle Olen after he left. My mama and daddy always said everyone wanted to believe he got free."

Miriam was so confused. Was Joe filling Cissy's head with a bunch of falsehoods? And if he was, should Miriam tell her?

～✺～

Two days before Passover, Miriam was working on her lessons while Bubby unpacked the boxes of supplies that Bart had brought up from the storage room to the kitchen. Concentrating on arithmetic was a challenge with the steady stream of dishes, pots, pans and linens piling up around her. It was hard not to feel a bit of excitement.

Finally, Miriam put down her pencil and looked at her grandmother. "Bubby, I was thinking about what you said when we were in Utica, about how you don't have to be Jewish to go to a seder. Do you suppose Tante Malka knows that?"

Bubby was examining a lace tablecloth. It was nicer than anything Miriam had seen since arriving at the farm. "Those New York apartments are awfully small. I don't imagine Malka has much room for more than her relatives," she said, flicking away a loose thread. "But I'm sure she knows that everyone is welcome at a seder. It says so in the *Haggadah*. 'Let all who are hungry come and eat. Let all who are needy come and celebrate Passover.' It's traditional to have strangers join us."

Bubby handed Miriam a rag and pointed at a cabinet in the corner of the kitchen. "If you're not going to work on your lessons, take this and dust the shelves. They need to be clean for the

Pesach dishes," she said, using the Hebrew word for the holiday.

"The hired men aren't really strangers," Miriam said as she dragged the rag over the middle shelf. "You know them."

"That's true," Bubby agreed. "But you never know when a stranger might appear." She handed Miriam a box of silver polish. "When you're done with the shelf, you can start shining the seder plate and the silver."

"There's so much," Miriam said. Once she started, she might never get out of the house.

"You'll still have time to visit the kittens," Bubby said. "Have you decided which one to keep?"

"Star, I think," Miriam said.

"Not Moses? It would be fitting to have a Moses at our seder."

"Star is friendlier," Miriam said, which was true. Moses was so devoted to Cissy that Miriam couldn't even lure him away to play with a piece of yarn.

Miriam had been thinking a lot about the conversation the previous week. She really wanted to tell Cissy what Franklin and Joe had said about the Underground Railroad. It felt dishonest to keep the story from her. She deserved to know that the uncle she and Joe were looking for hadn't come to New York on a real train and had likely passed away many years ago. But she could not think of how to put a happy ending on it. If she told Cissy, either she would make her angry or, worse, cause her to lose hope.

Still, it troubled Miriam that Joe had not told Cissy the truth. If only Cissy weren't so determined to remain hidden! Miriam wished all the secrets could be out in the open. Later that afternoon, when Bubby said she had done enough for now, she raced to the barn. Cissy heard the door opening and poked her head out of the stall with the kittens, greeting her with an enthusiastic, "Down here!"

Suddenly Miriam had an idea. By the time she was face-to-face with Cissy, she was convinced she had come up with the perfect solution. She felt sure Cissy would feel the same way.

"You can come to our seder!" she announced.

Cissy gave her a chilly look.

"What are you talking about?" she asked.

"The seder—remember, the holiday? Passover?"

"'Course I remember that," Cissy said, her eyes narrowing. "But I ain't coming to your dinner. I'm a secret. How many times do I have to tell you?"

"Bubby just told me that we're supposed to invite a stranger to the seder. We don't have any strangers, just the hired men, and they're not strangers because we know them. So *you* can be the stranger! You can come! You have to!"

Cissy shook her head. "I told you, I can't go into the house."

"But you can!" Miriam insisted. "You can knock on the door and say you're lost. I'll pretend I don't know you."

Cissy was still shaking her head. "Joe will know me."

Miriam was beginning to doubt her brilliant idea. She had forgotten about Joe and his threats of the orphanage. She kept talking, though, hoping she could change Cissy's mind.

"You are crazy," Cissy said. She sounded as unfriendly as she had the first time she spoke to Miriam.

How quickly a good idea could turn into a bad one. All you needed was to lose faith. *Sometimes thinking something's as powerful as doing something.* That's what Cissy had said.

But Cissy was so afraid, she would hear no talk about coming into Bubby and Zayde's house.

"You're as much a scaredy-cat as I am," Miriam blurted out.

Cissy looked as if Miriam had struck her. "What do you mean by that?" she demanded.

"You're afraid to come to the seder because you think you're going to be sent to an orphanage. Bubby and Zayde wouldn't let that happen."

Cissy was about to reply when the barn door groaned open.

The girls heard Zayde's booming voice. "Where's my Miri?" he called out cheerfully. "C'mon, my *shayna maydel*! Let's choose your kitten and get back into the house!"

TWENTY-ONE

When Zayde's voice filled the barn, Miriam forgot that Cissy was beside her. She turned toward the door to call out, "I'm here, in the stall." But Cissy, now standing behind her, reached out and covered her mouth. Miriam couldn't speak. She could barely breathe.

"Miri?" Zayde called again.

Miriam wanted to respond—she did not want her grandfather to worry. She pulled at Cissy's hand, but Cissy's grip was too strong.

You're hurting me, she thought.

"Miri?" Zayde called out again. "Where's my Miri? Bubby said you were in here." His voice grew louder as he neared the stall.

It occurred to Miriam that there was a way to free herself. She opened her mouth, preparing to chomp on the soft part of Cissy's palm. Maybe Cissy sensed it, because she suddenly yanked her hand away and pushed Miriam toward the door.

"Go!" she said.

Miriam planted her feet firmly on the ground and refused to move.

Cissy whispered more insistently. "I said *go! Get out of here!*" Her hands were on Miriam's shoulders when the stall door opened and Zayde rushed in. Cissy immediately dropped her hands to her sides. Zayde had started to speak, but when he saw Cissy behind Miriam, his sentence ended at "What?" His mouth hung open as he looked from Miriam to Cissy and back again. When he found his voice, it was louder than anything Miriam had ever heard from him.

"What is this? Who are you? And what are you doing to my granddaughter?"

Miriam backed up so she was standing next to Cissy. She reached for Cissy's hand to show her grandfather that she was safe, even though only moments ago she had been very scared. But she knew Cissy had been just as scared. She was certain Cissy still was.

"This is Cissy," Miriam said. "She's my stranger."

Zayde's tone softened, but only slightly. "Your *what*?"

"Bubby said we're supposed to welcome strangers to the seder. Cissy is my stranger."

Zayde sank down onto a hay bale and cradled his head in his hands. Cissy looked at Miriam and put her hand over her heart. That's when Miriam noticed that she was shivering.

I'm sorry, Cissy mouthed.

Miriam shook her head. "You don't have to worry," she whispered. "Nothing bad is going to happen."

❧

They walked back to the house quickly, Cissy wearing Zayde's warm overcoat. Miriam wanted to tell Zayde everything right away, but he shushed her. "Tell it once, to your bubby and me at the same time. Then we hear the same story."

Bubby was in the kitchen, polishing the rest of the silverware, her back to the door. "Did you bring the kitten?" she asked, turning around as they entered the room. When she saw Cissy, she leaned backward against the kitchen counter to steady herself. "Who is this?" she asked, making no effort to hide her surprise.

"This is Miriam's stranger," Zayde said. "Apparently, you told her we invite a stranger to the seder. So she has found a stranger. This is all I know. We will hear the rest of the story now. Sit, everyone."

Miriam took her usual seat at the kitchen table. She motioned for Cissy to sit next to her. Despite the many times she had imagined presenting Cissy to her grandparents, she was momentarily tongue-tied. She didn't know where to begin, so she looked to Cissy for guidance. Cissy shook her head.

"It's your story," she said quietly.

"If no one is going to speak, then I will ask a question," Zayde said, turning to Cissy. "Where did you come from?" he asked gently. "And how did you find our barn?"

"She's Joe's sister," Miriam explained.

"You mean—you mean you've been living in the barn since the harvest?" Zayde was flabbergasted.

Cissy nodded. "In the loft. Joe said we were just going to stay until we could find our uncle. He lives somewhere in New York."

Miriam thought about what Franklin had said and hoped her grandparents wouldn't ask Cissy too many questions about this uncle. She was grateful when Zayde put a hasty end to the conversation.

"Eva, get the girl something warm to eat and drink," he said to Bubby. "I'll go find Joe."

As soon as Zayde left the house, Bubby went to the stove and began heating milk for cocoa. Cissy began shivering again. Miriam moved her chair closer and rubbed her shoulders. Bubby placed a plate of cookies and the hot cocoa in front of her.

"There's nothing to be afraid of," Bubby assured her.

"She thinks you're going to send her to an orphanage," Miriam said.

Cissy shook her head. "Joe's going to be so mad at me." She looked at Miriam. "I promised him I didn't talk to you. That first day in the barn, when you tried climbing into the loft—" A hint of a smile brightened her eyes for just a second, and then her face went dark again.

Miriam stole a look at her grandmother, but Bubby didn't seem the least bit surprised, or even angry, to hear that she had attempted the ladder. Bubby was completely focused on Cissy.

"I told him I didn't know you," Cissy continued. "I lied to him, and you lied to your granny and grandpa." Tears began rolling down her cheeks. "I am so sorry."

Bubby motioned for Miriam to move to the next chair, to make room for her to sit next to Cissy. When she sat down, she pulled Cissy close, wrapping her in a gentle hug. "There's no need to worry, *bubeleh*. Your brother just wanted to keep you safe. But you will be safer here than you were in the barn. And warmer too. Now come, shhhh. Stop your tears."

TWENTY-TWO

Bubby and Zayde didn't want anyone knowing that Cissy had been living in the loft. "We can't have people thinking that is acceptable," Zayde said, which was as close as he came to scolding Joe in front of Cissy and Miriam. "At dinner, we will introduce Cissy as your sister who's staying with us until you find your relatives. If they ask when she arrived, we will say she rode the train. That is true. They need know nothing more."

"Do you have any information at all about this uncle?" Zayde asked Joe. "A name? An idea of what year he came north?" He paused. "One night at dinner you talked about the Underground

Railroad. Is that how this relative you're planning to find traveled up north?"

Cissy, who had been looking sleepy through most of the conversation, suddenly sat at attention, her eyes sharpened on her brother. "Are you talking about Uncle Olen? The one that escaped back in 1850-something? *That's* the uncle we come up here to find? How are we going to find some uncle that's been dead longer than we been alive? Are you crazy or something?"

Joe put his fingers to his lips. "Get a hold of yourself, Cissy," he said. "I ain't crazy. There is some kin of Mama's up here, Willis or Williams or some such. I was only a boy when I met him. He was moving to New York to be a musician. He came by the house on his way up north. You don't remember. You were too young. But he could play trumpet like nobody's business."

Cissy's eyes burned into Joe. "You're telling me the uncle we're looking for you met only one time? And that he ain't even our uncle! Why'd you tell me we had an uncle up here anyhow?"

"We did," Joe said. "Uncle Olen." He paused and looked at her, guilty. "I'm sorry. I didn't lie to you. I ain't never going to lie to you. But I wasn't straight with you neither. It was the only way I could get you to leave Auntie May and Uncle Hesh. And we had to get out of there. You know that."

Cissy nodded, seeming to understand. But then she turned angry again. "How in blazes are we going to find some man you only met one time? And when you were so little you don't even remember his name proper?"

Joe hung his head. When he faced his sister again, he looked as scared as Cissy had when Zayde had burst into the stall. "I don't rightly know," he admitted. "I still haven't figured that part out."

He turned to Bubby and Zayde. "I'm sorry for all the trouble." Then he looked at Cissy. "We can't stay here anymore," he said, head hanging down again. "We'll have to move on."

Cissy and Miriam began to protest at the same time, but they were drowned out by the sound of Bubby's sensible, measured voice. "You will do nothing of the sort." She was still sitting between the girls, and she laid her arm protectively over Cissy's shoulders. "There's no reason for you to leave. You're a good worker. There's plenty for you to do here. Cissy can stay with us until you have found a proper home."

And so it was settled. Bubby and Zayde even offered to give Cissy her own room. But Miriam and Cissy agreed they would rather share. Zayde and Joe moved a bed in from the spare room. They placed it against the wall opposite Miriam's bed.

"Anything is better than sleeping with cows," Cissy admitted late that night, after lights-out. "But this is really nice."

Miriam squinted, trying to bring her into focus, but the room was too dark. "Wait a minute," she said. She pushed open the curtains, letting the moon light up the room.

Cissy had rolled onto her side and was propped on her elbow, facing Miriam. "I told you it wasn't so bad, sleeping in the loft, but sometimes at night when it was especially windy, I'd feel like the roof was going to blow right down on my head. And there were critters up there."

"Critters?" Miriam said.

"Mice. Rats. I don't know. Little four-legged crawly things with fur. I only saw them once or twice. Mostly I'd hear all this pitter-pattering in the hay. It was creepy. That's why I started bringing Moses up there, 'cause he'd chase them away. Or eat them."

Miriam cringed. "They were there when I was there with you?"

"Yeah," Cissy said. "Remember that time you heard something scratching and you thought maybe it was Anna and Ida and I said yes? But they were down in the stall with the rest of the kitties. I just didn't want to tell you."

"That was critters?" Miriam made a face and shuddered. "Ewww."

Cissy laughed. "What are you *ewwwing* about? You sleep in this nice room in a real bed, and you didn't even know there was anything to be scared of until I just told you."

"What a good friend you are!" Miriam teased her.

Cissy turned serious. "So are you."

~

Miriam woke the next morning to a strange, growly sound. At first she thought it was a kitten, but they were all in the barn. Then she rolled over and saw the lump under the covers on the other bed. That's when she remembered the events of the day before, and a big grin spread over her face. She really wanted to wake Cissy. But Cissy was sleeping so peacefully, under warm covers, in a bed, for the first time in who knew how long. Miriam quietly climbed out of her bed and tiptoed across the floor toward the door.

"Where are you going?" Cissy was sitting up, rubbing her eyes. Her hair was sticking out at odder angles than usual.

"I didn't want to wake you," Miriam said.

"I don't sleep too soundly," Cissy said. "Couldn't in the barn, can't here."

Miriam didn't want to tell her how loud she'd been snoring. She was just happy her friend had slept well. "Let's get dressed so we can go downstairs. Passover starts tomorrow. I'm sure Bubby has lots for us to do."

TWENTY-THREE

After breakfast Bubby put the girls to work cracking walnuts while she peeled apples.

"Is that charoses you're making, ma'am?" Cissy asked.

"Now how do you know about charoses?" Bubby replied with a big smile.

"Miriam told me all about the seder, ma'am," Cissy said. "I know about the mortar and the salt water and the horseradish sandwich. I ain't so sure I want to eat any horseradish though."

"It's just a taste, Cissy," Miriam reminded her. "You have to. It's part of the seder."

Cissy shrugged. "I suppose. If I have to."

There was only one nutcracker, so Miriam and Cissy divided the work. Cissy cracked the nuts, and Miriam fished out the meat. She placed the shells in one bowl and the nuts in another.

"You missed some there," Cissy said, pointing at the shell Miriam had just dropped into the bowl. "See?"

Miriam retrieved the shell and inspected it more closely. Sure enough, there was a hunk of nut left inside. "You're better at this than I am," she said.

"My mama made the best pecan pie in Whiskey Corner," Cissy said. "I cracked the nuts while she made the crust." She took a deep breath, then let out a sigh. "You know how people say 'that crust is so good it melts in your mouth'?"

Miriam nodded.

"Mama's crust really did melt in your mouth," Cissy said.

Miriam reached for the nutcracker. "Let's trade jobs," she said.

When the girls finished with the nuts, they worked on putting the rest of the Passover dishes and cookware in the cabinet. It took ages, because Cissy insisted on inspecting each item.

"I don't understand," she said as she ran her fingers over the gold rim of an ivory-colored dinner plate. "These are so pretty, and you only use them for one week of the year, not every day?" She shook her head. "If that ain't crazy, I don't know what is."

"We use different dishes and silverware and pots and pans for Passover because we eat different foods for that one week," Bubby explained. "During the rest of the year we eat food that can rise, like bread, but on Passover—"

Cissy broke in. "I know. You can't. Because the Israelites had to skedaddle out of Egypt in a hurry, so you have to eat flat, crunchy stuff all week. Miriam told me everything."

Miriam beamed.

"It's part of what makes the holiday special," Bubby went on. "The food we eat is special, and so we use special pots and pans and dishes and silver-ware too."

Cissy nodded thoughtfully. "I understand," she said. "At my granny's house when I was little, at Christmas and Easter she always served up the ham on a special plate. She never used it except for holidays. And sometimes birthdays." She paused. Miriam thought she looked a little sad. "I'd forgot about that until just now."

"So it's not so crazy after all?" Miriam said, giving her a light punch on the shoulder.

"No, it's nice," Cissy agreed.

Bubby handed the girls aprons. "Cissy, now we're going to teach you how to make matzah balls," she said. "You'll both need to wash your hands."

"They're just going to get messy all over again though," Miriam informed her. "Matzah balls are messy."

Bubby set a basket of eggs and a large blue bowl in front of the girls. "All right. First I need you to crack twelve eggs into the bowl," she said. "Can you do that without getting any shells in the mix, Cissy?"

"Oh yes, ma'am," Cissy replied. "But I need to use a knife to do it right."

Bubby raised her eyebrows but handed her a paring knife. Cissy brought the knife down onto the center of the eggshell, splitting it perfectly in two. Miriam picked up a knife and tried to do the same, but her egg splintered, and she had to pick bits of shell out of the bowl.

"You need to hit it more clean," Cissy said. "Don't be afraid. Watch me." Miriam mimicked Cissy's sure movements and soon got the hang of it. In a minute the bowl was filled with eggs— without their shells. Bubby added cooking oil and chicken stock, and Miriam mixed it together with a wooden spoon. Then Bubby added a box of matzah meal to the liquid, and Cissy stirred the thick mixture one last time.

"So we make the balls now?" she asked.

"First it has to chill," Bubby said, sliding the bowl into the icebox. "Otherwise it's impossible to work with."

Bubby and the girls then got to work peeling carrots and potatoes for the *tzimmes*. By the time they had finished chopping the vegetables and emptying them into a cast-iron pot with prunes and apricots, the matzah-ball mix was firm enough to work with. Bubby took it out of the icebox and placed it back on the table.

"First you have to coat your hands with cooking oil," Miriam advised Cissy.

Cissy looked skeptical.

"Trust me," Miriam said. "Otherwise it will be like having glue on your hands all day. You can wash the oil off afterward."

Miriam spooned up a blob of matzah meal about the size of a silver dollar and shaped it into a ball with her hands. Then she carefully dropped it into the pot of boiling water on the stove. Cissy did the same. "You're right," Cissy said as she formed another ball. "It feels like sand. Kind of reminds me of that hamen hat you gave me that time."

"Matzah balls are nothing like hamantaschen," Miriam promised her.

~∽~

On the way to the barn after lunch, the wind stung Miriam's face. She covered her nose and mouth with one mittened hand to keep warm.

"When did it get so cold?" she asked, but the mitten muffled her voice. Even if it hadn't, Cissy probably wouldn't have heard. She was too busy chattering away. She was excited because Bubby had told the girls that they could each pick a kitten to come live in the house.

"You are so lucky you got that granny," Cissy said. "She is so kind to everyone. Joe said she was, but I don't think I expected her to be quite the way she is."

"I tried to tell you too," Miriam reminded her.

Cissy didn't respond right away. Miriam worried that she had hurt her friend's feelings.

"Because I didn't want you to keep living out here," she added. "I was worried about you."

Cissy put her hand on Miriam's shoulder. "I know," she said. "I believe you now. You said they wouldn't send me away, and you were right. But sometimes a person has to see for themselves. Everybody's got their own way of doing things."

"I know," Miriam said.

When they reached the barn, Miriam suggested one last trip up to the loft.

·"Why?" Cissy asked.

"Isn't there anything you want from up there? The blanket, maybe? Or, I don't know, Joe's shirt?"

Cissy shook her head. "That shirt's been eaten to death. It's got more holes than the colander your granny was using to wash her apples this morning. And the blanket was rougher than twine and about as useful. The critters can have at 'em. Let's see the cats and then go back to the house where it's warm."

Cissy stopped when they reached the stall door. She turned to Miriam. "I'm sorry I hurt you yesterday."

Miriam almost said, "You didn't," but she stopped herself. The truth was, Cissy *had* hurt her.

"I was going to bite your hand if you didn't stop covering my mouth," Miriam admitted.

Cissy looked disbelieving. "You were *not!*"

"I was," Miriam said, pushing open the stall door.

Cissy looked down at her hands. "I guess I saved myself just in time," she said.

Moses was perched on top of the pile of hay bales, inspecting his paws. Anna and Ida were bickering nearby. The girls found Bandit and Socks lounging in the trough with MC, but they had to flatten themselves on the floor to locate Pirate and Star. The kittens were hiding under the trough, almost in the next stall.

"Come on, kitty," Miriam said, trying to lure Star with a piece of twine. "Come on out so I can take you to your new home!"

Star took the twine in her paws, and Miriam began slowly pulling it toward her, until she was able to reach the kitten and scoop her up.

"You sure you don't want Anna or Ida?" Cissy asked.

"No," Miriam said. "I want Star."

"'Cause she's pretty as a star?" Cissy teased.

Miriam smiled. "That is precisely why."

TWENTY-FOUR

Miriam thought there had been enough surprises on the farm to last a lifetime, but she and Cissy were greeted with another when they left the barn. In the short time they'd been inside, the temperature had dropped even more. And snow was falling so fast and hard they could barely find the path to the house.

"Jiminy!" Cissy said, tucking Moses into her jacket as she whirled in a circle, her face turned toward the sky. "It's like the world's disappeared!" She held out her free hand and watched the flakes pile up on the mittens Bubby had given her.

"Is this the first time you've seen snow?" Miriam asked, cuddling Star close.

"I saw it yesterday and today, what little there was out here when we were going back and forth to the house. But I ain't never seen it coming down like this."

Miriam wished she was as excited as Cissy, but the snow made her homesick all over again. Even if it wasn't warm at this time of the year, there was still the promise of spring back home. "It's not supposed to snow on Passover," she said, not caring how glum she sounded. "Snow happens in the winter."

"Tell that to the snow!" Cissy said. She sounded as happy as Miriam had ever heard her, and her mood was catching. "Come on, cheer up!" Cissy stuck out her tongue, waited for the snow to land on it and pulled it back in with a satisfied smile. "It tastes good! Stop bellyaching and try some!"

~∽

"We get *meshugganah* weather here upstate," Zayde said, sitting in the front room after dinner that night with Bubby, Miriam and Cissy. They had invited Joe to stay with them, but he had declined. He clearly did not feel as comfortable in the house as his sister did. He stayed slightly longer than the rest of the hired men, but after promising to see Cissy at breakfast, he returned to the bunkhouse.

The snow was still coming down. "Sometimes on Passover it's hot as summertime, and every once in a while it snows," Zayde continued. "It's a special treat for Miriam, for her first Passover with her bubby and zayde. And for you, Cissy. I bet you've never seen snow on Passover."

"I ain't never seen Passover, sir," Cissy said with a giggle. "So it's all new to me."

Miriam was about to suggest that they build a snow fort the next day. But there was a knock at the door, and Mazel started barking. Usually the dog slept outside, but it was so cold that Zayde had brought him into the house. Now he ran toward the door, his ears perked up, his tail wagging.

"Who could that be?" Bubby wondered as she and Zayde made their way down the hall.

Ordinarily, people only showed up at the house after a train passed. But the last train had sped by during supper. The next wasn't due until the middle of the night.

Miriam followed her grandparents through the kitchen. Between the snow and the darkness, she wondered how anyone could have found the front door at all.

She was about to say so when she realized that Cissy was no longer with her. She went back into the front room. She saw Cissy on the sofa, frozen like a statue. A scared statue.

"They're coming for me," she whispered in a voice so soft Miriam had to lean in to hear her. "From the orphanage. You said your granny and grandpa wouldn't tell. I believed you. But they did. And now someone's coming to get me. You have to hide me! Now!"

She clamped onto Miriam's hand with the same powerful grip she'd used to cover her mouth the day before. This time, though, Miriam wasn't afraid.

"Nobody told anyone anything, Cissy," she said, taking her place on the sofa beside her friend.

"There are no orphanages here." She did her best to sound firm, the way Mama did when she was saying something important. Even as she spoke, though, Miriam realized she didn't know if what she was saying was true. All she knew was that she had never seen or heard of an orphanage in Sangerfield or Waterville.

Instead of admitting as much, she told Cissy the one thing she was sure of. "Bubby and Zayde haven't left the farm since yesterday."

"The hired men then. Somebody told!" Cissy bolted off the sofa. "I have to get out of here." She looked toward the windows, then back at Miriam, her eyes pleading. "Ain't you going to come with me?"

"Don't even think of going outside," Miriam warned. "You'll freeze. You'll never find the barn in this snow. Just go upstairs. Hide under the bed if that makes you feel safe. I'll stay here, and if whoever is at the door really is someone who's going to take you away, I'll come up and we'll figure something out."

She wanted to add, "You don't have to worry," but Cissy was gone.

∽

Miriam couldn't see who Zayde and Bubby had let in, but it sounded like there was more than one person. Perhaps it was hobos after all—it wasn't unusual for them to arrive in groups.

But when the new visitors emerged from the hallway, behind Bubby and Zayde, Miriam knew right away that they weren't hobos. They were dressed in fancy city clothes, pressed slacks and button-down shirts with thin ties. Three of them were so tall and broad they filled the doorway. Two were barely taller than Bubby. All of them were black.

Miriam, remembering what her mama said about it not being polite to stare, quickly turned her attention to the stiff-looking cases the men were carrying. Most of the cases were shaped like rectangles. Some were nearly as long as a piano keyboard. The largest was bigger than Mazel's doghouse and taller than Miriam.

The men set the cases in a corner of the kitchen and stood quietly as Zayde introduced them.

"This is the Johnstown Jazz Band," he said. "They were on their way to Utica, but the snowstorm is too dangerous for driving, so they're going to stay here for the night."

"Here?" Miriam asked. In the house? She wondered how they would fit. Their cases alone took up most of the space in the kitchen. She wondered what instruments they played.

"In the bunkhouse with the hired men," Bubby explained. "But we're going to have a proper visit first."

"Are you going to play a concert?" Miriam asked.

The men laughed so loudly that Miriam was sure Cissy must have heard, even if she was hiding under the bed. One of them said, "Well, that is something we can do, if you like, miss."

"I'm going to go get Cissy," she announced.

"Where did she go?" Bubby asked.

"She—she just went upstairs," Miriam replied. She didn't want to tell her grandparents what Cissy was so scared of, especially not in front of strangers.

～

The room that the girls shared was dark, but Miriam could hear Cissy under the bed, her breath raggedy and quick. She obviously hadn't heard the men laughing—or maybe she had, and that had scared her even more. Miriam reached for the metal chain hanging from the ceiling, turning the light on.

"Come out, Cissy," she said, crouching down to look under the bed. Cissy still looked terrified. "They're not from an orphanage. They're musicians!"

"How do you know they're not lying?"

"They aren't," Miriam promised.

"You ask for proof?"

"They're carrying musical instruments," Miriam said. "The cases are so big. They're big enough for us to hide in."

As soon as the words were out, she realized her mistake. Cissy slid farther back. "That's to take me away. I ain't coming out."

"You're being silly," Miriam said. "They don't even know who you are. They don't even know you're here."

"Did you see the inside of the cases?" Cissy demanded. "Did you actually see any instruments?"

Miriam shook her head no, but Cissy couldn't see her from so far under the bed.

"Did you see the inside of the cases?" Cissy repeated. "Did you?"

"No!" Miriam said. "Now stop being ridiculous. Come out."

"Nobody's going to take *you* away—you got a mama and a papa to go back to," Cissy reminded her.

"Bubby and Zayde won't let anyone take you away," Miriam insisted. "And those men aren't here to take anyone away in the first place."

"Then how come they are here?" Cissy asked.

"The weather's too bad for them to drive to Utica," Miriam said.

"This ain't a hotel. How come they didn't find a hotel?"

"I don't know," Miriam said. "Maybe they saw the hobo mark." She knew that wasn't possible— it was too dark to see anything.

Cissy did not respond.

"They came to the door and Mazel started barking and Zayde said they're going to stay in the bunkhouse with the rest of the hired men," Miriam said. She drew herself up to her knees and then stood. "Fine. If you want to stay under there all night, go ahead. But I'm going back downstairs."

Cissy poked her head out from under the bed. Strains of music were floating up from the floor below. The men were playing after all! Miriam didn't recognize the tune, but it was so lively it seemed to have distracted Cissy from everything she'd been worrying about. Those few notes changed her entire mood. It was as if someone had cast a spell on her.

"See?" Miriam said. "They *do* have instruments!"

Cissy slid all the way out from beneath the bed and shook herself, the way Mazel did first thing in the morning. "Oh my goodness!" she said, standing in the bedroom doorway.

"What?" Miriam asked.

"My mama loved that song." She began swaying gently, then singing quietly, "*Two left feet, oh, so neat, has Sweet Georgia Brown.* We used to dance around the kitchen to that tune when I was little."

"You should go downstairs and sing with them," Miriam said.

Cissy shook her head. "Uh-uh," she said. "I'm staying here."

"They're not from an orphanage," Miriam promised. "Just come and see."

Cissy still looked doubtful—but not for the reason Miriam thought. "I haven't sung with anybody since before Joe and I came up here. And sometimes musicians don't want nobody singing with them anyhow."

"If they don't want you to sing, we'll come back upstairs and you can sing for me. But at least come down and say hello. Besides, Bubby was worried about you."

Miriam held out her hand, and together the two girls went downstairs.

TWENTY-FIVE

The snowstorm that had brought the Johnstown Jazz Band to the farm showed no signs of letting up. By the next afternoon, it was clear that the band members would be staying for dinner. There was no hotel in Sangerfield, the hotels in Waterville wouldn't give them a room, and the roads were still too dangerous. They had nowhere else to go.

The Passover that Miriam thought would be the loneliest ever was turning out to be anything but. As she polished the last of the silver, she hummed the melody to "Ma Nishtana," The Four Questions. The first question was, "Why is this night different from all other nights?" In the Haggadah, the answer was that it was different because on this night, on Passover, people ate unleavened bread. But standing in the kitchen, which was busier than Miriam had ever seen it, she could just as easily say it was different because it was truly going to be the most unusual, unexpected seder ever.

Joe and Bart were carting a table into the house to make room for the extra visitors, who were in the living room. They were playing music while Bubby, Miriam and Cissy cooked. The concert had been Bubby's idea.

"It's not often I have entertainment when I'm working in the kitchen," she said to Antoine. He was the shortest, and he played the biggest instrument, the double bass. He stood slightly behind and to the side of it, his left hand sliding up and down its long neck as his slender dark fingers pressed down on the strings. His right hand seemed to dance as it plucked out a melody that was unfamiliar to Miriam, but impossible to ignore. Cissy seemed to know most of the band's songs. "We used to do this all the time," she said. "Everybody in town would gather at someone's house on Friday for the hootenannies. Musicians would play all night long, and if you didn't have your own instrument, you could sing." She stopped talking and listened to the song from the next room. "That's 'Little Liza Jane.'" Tapping her fingers, Cissy began singing along.

"Just go in there and sing with them already," Miriam said, nudging her. "You know all the words."

Cissy shook her head. "I can sing just as well in here with you. Besides, you need my help."

Joe and Bart brought another table into the house. They were followed by Stretch, who was carrying a box so big Miriam wondered how he could see where he was going.

Bubby directed him to set the box down by the table. She asked Cissy to unpack it. Cissy reached in and pulled out a small pillow. "You want me to make a bed?" she asked. "In the kitchen?"

Bubby shook her head, smiling. "I want you to put one on everyone's chair," she said.

"Like this?" Cissy put a pillow on the seat of the chair closest to her. "Or this?" She propped the pillow against the chair back.

"Whichever you want," Miriam said. "People will figure out what's most comfortable. That's what they're for—because we're supposed to recline at the seder, to be comfortable."

Cissy nodded slowly, approvingly. "I like that idea."

Miriam went back to piling the last of the silverware on the counter. Next, she counted out sixteen bowls for soup and stacked them. Finally, she counted out plates for the gefilte fish.

"What are you smiling about?" Cissy asked.

"I thought this was going to be the loneliest seder ever," Miriam said. "But it's not. The best thing about Passover is having everyone together. And listening to the stories about Moses leading the Israelites out of Egypt and across the Red Sea. And looking for the *afikomen*."

"The what?"

"The afikomen. I thought I told you about it."

"I think I'd remember a word like that," Cissy said. "How come Moses was looking for the affy komin?"

Miriam laughed, shaking her head. "Moses didn't look for it. We do—me and all my cousins."

"What is it?" Cissy asked.

"It's a piece of matzah. This." Miriam pointed to a box of matzah on the kitchen counter. "The person leading the seder breaks off a piece and hides it, and then later we look for it. And whoever finds it wins a penny, or maybe a piece of candy, or sometimes even both."

"Do you play other games at the seder?" Cissy asked.

"Just hiding the afikomen," Miriam said. "But I was thinking it wasn't going to be very much fun looking for it all by myself. So that's another reason I'm happy you are here."

"Me too," Cissy said. She thought for a minute. "How long's this dinner, anyway, if you have to be hiding stuff and looking for it in the middle?"

"Long," Miriam said. "Sometimes I fall asleep before it's over, but it's hard to stay asleep because it's so noisy. Everybody's talking, and at the end everybody sings."

"I betcha you ain't going to be falling asleep tonight," Cissy said. "It's going to be extra noisy."

❧

The men arrived at the house at sunset, just in time for the seder.

"Are you going to play?" Miriam asked Antoine, who had left his double bass lying on its side in the living room.

"Not tonight, miss," Antoine said.

"Tonight it's your granny putting on a show, not us," added Felix, the trumpet player.

It was true. Bubby's table was a wonder, beautiful enough to rival Tante Malka's. Sitting atop the white lace tablecloth were the crystal glasses, ivory plates with gold rims and bowls of all different sizes. Some were filled with salt water and others with parsley to dip into the water. Others held charoses and horseradish. The seder plate took up most of the space in front of the chair where Zayde would sit. Atop the plate were a hard-boiled egg, a shank bone from a lamb and more parsley, horse-radish and charoses. Next to the seder plate was a small basket with three pieces of matzah, as flat and brown as sheets of corrugated cardboard.

Everyone gathered around the table. Miriam took the seat between Bubby and Cissy. Instead of sitting on the other side, facing Miriam, Joe squeezed in beside his sister. When he discovered the pillow on his chair, he couldn't hide his delight.

"Ain't this fancy!" he whispered, making himself comfortable.

Felix and Antoine sat opposite Cissy and Joe. Banjo sat farther down, next to Arthur, the saxophone player. As they leaned back against their pillows, Banjo peppered Arthur with questions. Miriam wondered if he would rather play in a band than work on a farm.

Zayde cleared his throat, a sign that the seder was about to begin.

"What's your grandpa doing?" Cissy asked Miriam. "Is he going to read during dinner?"

Before Miriam had a chance to answer, Zayde held up his book. "This is the Haggadah," he explained to Cissy and the rest of the guests. "It has been part of my family for many generations. It tells the story of Passover, and everything we have to do at the seder."

"That ain't English," Cissy said, pointing to the open page.

"It's Hebrew," Zayde said.

Cissy looked at Miriam. She spoke quietly. "You didn't tell me this was going to be in a different language."

"It's not—not all of it," Miriam replied. "Otherwise nobody here would understand."

Zayde looked around the table. "Welcome to our seder," he said. "Let all who are hungry come and eat. Let all who are needy come and celebrate Passover."

"Amen," Cissy said quietly. Miriam reached for Cissy's hand and held it.

Miriam had wondered how people who had never attended a seder could participate, especially when only Zayde had a Haggadah. At Tante Malka's, everyone had their own copy and could follow along. But it turned out that Zayde was such a good storyteller that nobody seemed to mind. He took care to explain each part of the service, starting with the food on the seder plate and the reason that the Israelites needed to escape from Egypt. When he explained how Moses first asked the pharaoh to free his people, Antoine and the other members of the band began tapping their fingers lightly on the table.

"Can we offer you a song?" they asked. When Zayde nodded, they began to sing. Miriam recognized the words that Cissy had sung in the barn, and she couldn't help but hum along. Joe and Cissy joined in, her voice soaring higher than the others.

When the song was over, everyone fell silent, looking admiringly at Cissy. "My goodness," said Felix. "You have a voice like an angel."

Cissy smiled. "Thank you," she said shyly.

When Zayde described the plagues, especially the river turning to blood and the frogs and locusts that overtook the land, Cissy looked at Joe. "You remember those locusts that summer when we was little?"

Joe shook his head. "Not now, Cissy," he mumbled. He seemed embarrassed.

"It's fine for Cissy to share," Bubby assured him. "Everyone participates, whether singing or telling a story. Go ahead, Cissy."

"I guess we had our own plague," Cissy said. "Those critters were everywhere—in the beds, in our clothes, even our food. But we didn't get out of there. We didn't have anywhere else to go. After a while, the locusts passed. Thanks be to God." She shuddered.

The dinner continued. Miriam could see that everyone was clearly having a good time. She overheard Antoine talking to Joe and Cissy. "You obviously got some good music in your family. And I hear you got kin somewhere in New York. He plays trombone? Or trumpet?"

"Trumpet," Joe said.

"What's his name? Maybe I know him."

"It's Willis," Joe said. "Or maybe Williams. Robert is his first name. But we haven't got an address or any idea where he's living. It's been a good ten years since we heard from him."

"We'll put the word out when we get back to Utica," Antoine said. "You never know. I can't be making any promises, but between the five of us, we work every end of New York State."

"You do that much gigging?" Joe asked.

Antoine shook his head. "A few nights a month. Rest of the time I'm a Pullman porter, and so are they." He nodded toward his bandmates. "We work between New York and Chicago, and we talk to plenty of people and lots of musicians. We'll do our best to help you find him."

"Thank you, sir," Joe said.

Cissy looked at Miriam, her face hopeful. "Thank you," she echoed.

One of Miriam's favorite parts of the seder came after the meal. That's when it was time to open the door for Elijah. Miriam had never opened the door—that honor was always reserved for one of her boy cousins. And every year the same thing happened. The cousin would open the door, and the hallway outside the apartment would be empty.

She wasn't sure what would happen if Elijah actually showed up. From what her parents said, it had something to do with the world becoming a better place, a place where everyone had a home that was safe and peaceful. It never made sense to Miriam that one person could do all that. It still didn't.

Zayde was getting ready to lead the blessing over the wine. That meant that soon it would be time for Miriam to open the door. She remembered what Cissy had said in the barn the first time they talked about Passover. *I don't think he's going to be coming to your house.* That had made Miriam angry, but it had also made her think. What she liked about the Elijah part of the seder was the stir of excitement and promise, when it was possible to believe that the great prophet just might be standing on the other side of the door. Maybe he'd take the time to drink his wine and join the family for a chorus of "Eliyahu Hanavi."

Zayde reached for the bottle of wine to fill Elijah's cup. As Miriam pushed her chair back from the table, a train rumbled past. She walked across the room and into the front hall and wondered if there were hobos on that train. She imagined opening the door not to Elijah, but to more travelers. Bubby and Zayde would find room and work for them and give them a home for as long as they needed.

She opened the door. Instead of being greeted by hobos or an ancient prophet, Miriam was hit with a blast of cold. When the frosty air cleared, she took in the snow-covered farmyard and the finally clear sky, blistered with stars.

No Elijah then, and not even more hired men. But this year, more than any other, she could feel reasons for hope. Mama and Papa were on their way home from the Old Country with Uncle Avram and Gabriel and Rafael. And she had a new friend, who would soon have a home of her own.

AUTHOR'S NOTE

Miriam's Secret is a work of fiction, but many of the details about Miriam's life come from my family's history. All four of my grandparents emigrated from eastern Europe in the early 1900s. My father's father was a teenager when he arrived in Boston in 1909. In 1921, three years after becoming a citizen of the United States, he returned to Lithuania to escort his mother, father and a younger brother to Boston, most likely saving them from certain death—twenty years later, the village where they had lived was burned to the ground by the Nazis.

My mother's father was also a teenager when he emigrated in 1906. At first he lived with an older sister on her chicken farm in New Jersey, then with an older brother in Central New York. Eventually he bought a horse and a cart and began working as a peddler, moving from town to town selling clothing and necessities at what we'd most likely recognize today as farmers' markets. After he'd saved enough money, he found a farm for sale, but the owner didn't want to sell to a Jewish person. My grandfather found someone else to handle the transaction.

When I was growing up, my family went to the farm almost every weekend. Sometimes my sister and I spent the night. Like Miriam, I was always shaken awake when a train thundered by. The seeds for *Miriam's Secret* were planted when my mother told me that hobos, as they were commonly referred to when she was growing up, used to jump off the trains and spend time working on the farm.

My grandfather once asked one of the men, *Why do so many of you come to my farm and not someone else's?* The man replied, *Your house is marked.* He wouldn't show my grandfather the mark though. No one would. Mom had no idea what it could have looked like.

When I began doing research for this story, I discovered that these migrant workers relied on a system of codes and symbols that warned their fellow travelers of danger, gave directions and indicated safe places to stay for a night. The mark on my grandparents' house likely said something to the effect of *Food here for work*.

Migrants weren't the only strangers who turned up at the farm. My aunt Freda told me that one wintry night a group of black jazz musicians performed a concert at the farmhouse. The men had been caught in a blizzard. They couldn't reach their intended destination, and no hotel would put them up. *Go see Billy the Jew*, they were told. *He'll give you a place to sleep.*

Mom had told me about the considerable anti-Semitism she and her siblings had faced growing up as the only Jewish family in the area, but I had never before heard my grandfather referred to that way.

In earlier drafts of this book, the scene where Miriam overhears the nickname the locals have for her grandfather was quite negative. But my perspective changed in early 2011, after my cousin Debbie Friedman died.

Debbie, who was Aunt Freda's daughter, was a pioneer in the world of Jewish liturgical music. Her untimely death received a lot of attention. Among the comments that appeared on the many obituaries published about her, I was struck by one that said something along the lines of *her grandparents were farmers in Sangerfield, New York. I think her grandfather was known as "Billy the Jew."* That was the first time it occurred to me that maybe there was a more benign explanation for Zayde's nickname. The comment helped me reframe that scene and, ultimately, the story.

No matter how far from home we travel or eventually settle, we never completely leave our origins behind—where we come from remains part of who we are. Identifying people based on their origins or background is natural—it's an easy form of classification. It's also linguistically clumsy and can be grating on the ears, but it's not necessarily ill-intentioned.

That said, I'm sure some people who referred to my grandfather as "Billy the Jew" did so out of racism, which existed at the turn of the nineteenth century for the same reasons it does today: ignorance and fear. The best way to overcome that ignorance and fear is also the same today as it was back then: by learning about and, if possible, getting to know people whose culture and origins are different from yours, identifying not merely what makes you different, but what you have in common.

The desire to create that kind of relationship for Miriam was, in part, what inspired Cissy. As far as I know, no child ever hid in my grandparents' hayloft, but Miriam needed a friend, and I've been fascinated with the idea of having a hidden friend from a different culture since reading *Summer of My German Soldier* by Bette Greene as a teenager.

The brief references to the Underground Railroad are a nod to Central New York's substantial role in the secret network in the late nineteenth century that enabled thousands of African Americans to escape enslavement in the American South. In fact, if you cross the railroad tracks that run alongside my grandparents' house and drive sixty-seven miles west on Route 20, you'll wind up in Auburn, NY, home and resting place of Underground Railroad "conductor" and American icon of courage, Harriet Tubman.

ACKNOWLEDGMENTS

If not for the stories that my mother and aunts told me about their life on the farm, there would be no Miriam. So thank you to the Chernoff sisters, Bessie Pollicove and Ann Binder (may their memories be for a blessing), Freda Friedman and Irlene Waldman, and their sister-in-law, Adele Kaye Chernoff Halligan, for sharing their memories with me. Thank you too to Phyllis Olshin Silverman, who was a child in Brooklyn in the 1930s and provided me with details about Miriam's life in the city.

I owe a big thanks to Robert Wuetherick, who set me straight on what it's like to grow up next to train tracks, and to David Makowsky at the Ukrainian Cultural Heritage Village in Alberta, who gave me free rein to poke around every barn on the property and treated me to a pierogi lunch as well. Thanks also to Otto Vondrak of the New York Central System Historical Society, Inc. for valuable information about pullman porters.

Lorie White, Caterina Edwards, Karen Spafford-Fitz, Lorna Schultz Nicholson, Eva Colmers and my sister, Amy Waldman, have lived with this story for nearly as long as I have, and I am grateful for their time, patience and advice.

Thanks also to the two people whose comments paved the way for Cissy: Christi Howes, who suggested that Miriam needed a friend, and Mar'ce Merrell, who gave me a much-needed kick in the literary pants when she looked at an early draft and said, *This is really beautiful, but nothing happens.*

Sophia Salamon is a reader after my own heart, and I thank her for her enthusiasm and helpful feedback. I hope to return the favor someday.

And finally, thanks to my family, Dave, Elizabeth, Noah and Chip, who provide me with more inspiration than they could possibly imagine.

DEBBY WALDMAN is the author of a number of children's books based on Jewish folktales, including *A Sack Full of Feathers*, which was named a 2007 Best Book for Kids and Teens by the Canadian Children's Book Centre, and *Clever Rachel*, declared by *Resource Links* to be one of the year's best for 2009. She is also the co-author of two books for parents of children who are hard of hearing. Debby lives in Edmonton, Alberta, with her husband, two children and a chocolate labradoodle named Chip. For more information, visit www.debbywaldman.com.